LONG WAY DOWN

Frank yanked open the door to the roof of the skyscraper. Joe and the security guards charged after him. Against the wind, Frank squinted at the chopper rising up from the roof. In the evening light he could make out Sarah in the front passenger seat.

"We're too late!" Frank heard one of the security guards shout. "They have her!"

Joe wasn't about to give up. He raced toward the helicopter and grabbed hold of its doorframe as it lifted away.

"Is he crazy?" the guard yelled. "He'll get killed!"

Joe struggled to enter the helicopter. Then he found himself facing the muzzle of a 9-mm Beretta.

"Let go, kid," growled the man in the chopper's backseat. "Let go or drop a hundred and twenty stories."

Books in THE HARDY BOYS CASEFILES® Series

THE HARDY BOYS CASEFILES NO. 72

SCREAMERS

FRANKLIN W. DIXON

AN ARCHWAY PAPERBACK
Published by POCKET BOOKS
New York   London   Toronto   Sydney   Tokyo   Singapore

This book is a work of fiction. Names, characters, places and incidents are either the product of the author's imagination or are used fictitiously. Any resemblance to actual events or locales or persons, living or dead, is entirely coincidental.

AN ARCHWAY PAPERBACK *Original*

An Archway Paperback published by
POCKET BOOKS, a division of Simon & Schuster Inc.
1230 Avenue of the Americas, New York, NY 10020

Copyright © 1993 by Simon & Schuster Inc.
Produced by Mega-Books of New York, Inc.

ISBN: 0-671-73108-4

First Archway Paperback printing February 1993

10 9 8 7 6 5 4 3 2 1

THE HARDY BOYS, AN ARCHWAY PAPERBACK and colophon are registered trademarks of Simon & Schuster Inc.

THE HARDY BOYS CASEFILES is a trademark of Simon & Schuster Inc.

Cover art by Brian Kotzky

Printed in the U.S.A.

IL 6+

SCREAMERS

Chapter

1

"A HUNDRED and twenty stories straight down," Joe Hardy said in a dramatic tone. The tall, blond seventeen-year-old pressed his forehead against the glass wall of the top-floor reception room and gazed down at Chicago's Christmas lights blinking in the twilight. "I knew computer software was big business, but I didn't know it could buy a building like this."

"Evanco doesn't just sell software," Joe's eighteen-year-old brother, Frank, said. "J. P. Evans started out building computers in the 1950s, but since then, his corporation has taken over dozens of smaller companies—newspapers, travel agencies, an airline, a few TV stations— you name it. And Evans himself is still one of the best-known computer whizzes on the planet. I can't believe you've never heard of the guy."

"If he owned a football team, maybe I would have," Joe joked. He turned and looked around the carpeted room. Large as it was, the space felt crowded by the one hundred fifty men and women clutching plastic glasses and trying to mingle as waiters in tuxedos offered hors d'oeuvres and music played softly over the speakers. "I don't know. It's just hard to imagine so many people who would pay to take a computer seminar when they work all day with computers. Seems kind of boring to me."

"But computers are taking over the world, Joe," Frank retorted, leaning against the glass wall. "You've got to get with the program."

Joe chuckled at Frank's unintended pun. Still, he found it hard to get as psyched up as Frank for this Christmas-vacation computer seminar. The subject of the seminar hosted by Evanco was computer security. Joe and Frank's father, a well-known private investigator, had been invited to give a talk on the new nationwide police records database now being introduced to law enforcement agencies. At the last minute, Fenton Hardy had asked his two sons to go along.

"Dad thought we'd want to line up some summer jobs, but there's no way I'd get hired by these guys," Joe said now as he watched their father, who was engaged in a deep discussion with a serious-looking man in his thirties. "Doesn't anyone who programs computers know how to have fun?"

"Not these days," Frank said. "Computer viruses have everyone in the business scared. A

2

computer can catch a virus through a floppy disk or electronic mail. And once it does, bang! The entire system breaks down. Corporations like Evanco hire dozens of programmers to set up new password systems and antivirus programs— and still the hackers who invent the viruses find ways to work around them."

Joe nodded vaguely. "Dad told me that a bunch of different computers have been going bust lately."

"Some of them actually exploded while people were working on them," Frank confided to him. "Evanco's computer network, EXacT, has been the hardest hit. Dad thinks Evanco's hosting this seminar so they can take advantage of the security sector's best brains. That man Dad's talking to is probably an Evanco employee—scared that if he doesn't come up with some kind of defensive action this week he might lose his job."

"This is just the opening reception," Joe protested. "Life's too short to worry every minute about getting fired."

Frank's eyebrows shot up. "It looks like there are at least two people here who agree with you."

Joe followed his brother's gaze to a pair of laughing young women standing near the elevators. They looked only slightly older than the Hardys. One was short and a little plump, with a thick mane of blond hair; the other was taller and lankier, with wavy, dark brown hair and sparkling green eyes that transfixed Joe from all the way across the room.

Joe eyed the two girls appreciatively. "They're dressed too well to work on computers," he decided. "Let's find out what they're up to."

With Frank trailing behind, Joe walked up to the two girls, who were wiping tears of laughter from their eyes. "Don't tell me," he said, grinning. "You're laughing at the idea that *this* is considered a hip way to spend an evening."

"Not exactly," the blond said. "You didn't see what just happened over there? Someone's beeper went off, and practically *every* person in the room checked his watch or his pocket or his briefcase." She and the other girl began laughing again. "Who are you, anyway?" the blond asked.

"Frank and Joe Hardy." Frank reached out to shake her hand. "We're here with our dad," he explained as he shook hands with the brunette girl. "I don't get it, though. What's so funny about checking your beeper?"

Joe and the two girls laughed again. "Just ignore my brother," Joe told them. "We're supposed to be hunting down summer jobs in Evanco's computer security division, and he's practicing being serious. What's your excuse for being here?"

"The same as yours," the brunette said with a smile. "Or mine is, at least. My name's Paulette, and this is Sarah. Rumor has it that the top brass in the industry are going to show up at this seminar. Sarah promised to introduce me to them. That way, when I finish college I can walk right into a cushy office at a company like Evanco, preferably with a Lake Michigan view. Right, Sarah?"

"Anything for a roommate," Sarah agreed, smiling at Frank. "It's no problem for me," she added. "I've known a lot of these people since I was a toddler."

"Why is that?" Frank asked. "Don't tell me you're a programming child prodigy."

Sarah laughed self-consciously. "Paulette's the prodigy. I'm just your average second-unit worker. But I'll give you a hint," she said. "My last name is Evans."

Joe stared at her. "You're J.P.'s daughter?"

"His *only* daughter," Paulette pointed out. "Practically everything Sarah knows about the computer business—and that's plenty—she learned at J.P.'s knee. I lucked out, didn't I, having her for a best friend."

"Speaking of which," Sarah said, taking her roommate by the arm, "if we don't start mingling, your career will be over before it begins." She turned to Frank and Joe. "Have fun, guys."

"Right." Joe sighed as the girls moved away. Paulette's emerald green eyes had a wonderful way of crinkling at the corners when she smiled, he thought. "If I'd known computer science experts could look like that, I'd have signed up for classes a long time ago," he remarked to his brother. "Let's get something to eat."

Frank followed Joe to the buffet table near the

bar. "I still can't believe it," Frank said, shaking his head. "J. P. Evans's only daughter! She must be worth billions."

"Watch out, Frank," his brother said. "Remember—Callie's waiting for you back home in Bayport."

"Of course I haven't forgotten Callie," Frank retorted. "It's just that—imagine growing up with Evans for a father. A guy that brilliant and powerful must expect a lot from his kids."

"You're probably right." Joe turned to see Fenton Hardy standing behind them, grinning. "But then, my kids rarely let me down," Fenton Hardy said.

Joe laughed. "Sorry, Dad. We were talking about J. P. Evans. We just met his daughter, Sarah."

"So I noticed," Mr. Hardy said. "But I doubt those girls are the ones to ask for summer jobs."

"Give us time, Dad," Joe protested. "We're still identifying all the players."

"Well, they're certainly here." Mr. Hardy glanced past his sons at the crowded room. "That new virus must have hit more companies than I realized. The biggest names in computers are in this room—all except Evans himself, that is. Did his daughter tell you whether he planned to be here tonight?"

"We didn't get a chance to ask," Joe admitted.

Mr. Hardy frowned. "I'll tell you what. I'll introduce you to a few fellows here and then—" He stopped midsentence as he saw something happening behind Joe. "What's going on?"

Joe followed his father's gaze to see that Sarah and Paulette had been joined across the room by two men. In spite of the fact that the men wore suits, Joe could see that they were no computer executives. The man on the girls' right was big and burly, with muscles that strained the seams of his jacket. The man on the left wore a black eyepatch and was poking a gun into Sarah's side.

"Hey!" Joe shouted.

Paulette screamed as the heavier thug pushed her to the ground, then joined his companion in hustling Sarah across the room. Other seminar participants turned and stared, stunned, as Sarah kicked at her assailants.

"Help!" Sarah shouted as the two men dragged her along.

Suddenly all three Hardys sprang into action. They raced toward the girl, with a dozen other men following behind. Just then the thug with the eyepatch spun around and aimed his gun at the crowd. "Everyone freeze!" he shouted in a gruff voice. "Come any closer and I'll shoot!"

Joe and Frank froze instantly, as did their father and the men behind him.

"What should we do?" Joe asked his brother in a low voice, keeping his eyes on the gun, which he noted was a .45 automatic.

"Nothing," Joe heard their father stage-whisper from behind them. "Security will take care of this. You boys stay clear."

Joe frowned as he watched the kidnappers half-drag, half-carry Sarah Evans toward the bank of elevators. He saw Sarah's pleading gaze directed at his brother and him. There's no way we're going to stand by and let them take her, he thought. He was aware of Paulette standing, fists clenched, to one side of the room.

Just then Joe heard Frank's voice, barely audible in his ear. "How about fourteen zulu?" Frank asked.

Joe nodded, his pulse speeding up with excitement. Fourteen zulu was a Bayport High School football play. "Stagger blitz?" he murmured.

"Yep," Frank said. Joe wondered if the other kidnapper was armed. So far he'd been content to keep an iron grip on Sarah Evans's arms.

Keeping their eyes on the crowd, the two men moved slowly with Sarah to the elevator bank. From close range, Joe could see that the burly kidnapper was even taller than he'd thought. There was something strange about their faces, Joe noted—both men's skin seemed unusually dark and smooth.

As the man with the eyepatch pressed the button for the elevator, Joe glanced toward his brother. "Move!" he yelled.

In a single movement, Frank and Joe charged forward just as the elevator doors slid open. Joe grunted as his shoulder collided with the abdomen of the gunman wearing the eyepatch. He heard the man gasp as the air was knocked out of him. There was a thud on the carpet, and Joe looked down to see the .45.

"I've got it, Joe!" Frank yelled, leaping for the gun as the crowd of onlookers murmured in shock and horror. Joe started toward Sarah, but just then the man with the eyepatch staggered back to his feet, spun Joe around, and punched him in the jaw. Joe went reeling backward into the crowd.

Dazed, Joe let himself bounce off the bodies of the onlookers and stagger back into the fray. No one in the crowd moved to help him, and Joe soon realized why: Frank and the second kidnapper were now battling over the gun. As the muzzle swung in all directions, many of the terrified onlookers fell to the floor.

"Joe!" Joe heard Paulette scream from somewhere in the crowd. "Get Sarah—quick!"

Joe swung toward the elevator. Sarah stood inside, her arms pinned behind her by the man with the eyepatch. She was struggling desperately to free herself.

"Hold on, Sarah!" His head buzzing, Joe staggered toward the elevator as the doors began to close. He leapt between the closing doors and lunged at the man holding Sarah. But the man was prepared. Sarah screamed as the kidnapper kicked Joe in the stomach, pushing him back out onto the carpet.

"They're getting away!" Joe heard Paulette's voice through a veil of pain as he fell to the floor. Dimly he was aware of a gun going off. Then he saw the burly kidnapper racing into the elevator.

Joe forced himself back onto his feet just in time to see the elevator doors close all the way. Joe rushed toward them again, joined by Frank and his father, but already he could hear the sound of the elevator moving.

"Joe," Joe heard his father say as though from a long distance away. "Are you all right?"

"Yeah," Joe said, looking down at his hand where he had grabbed at the kidnapper's face. There was something stuck to his fingers. With a growing sense of horror, Joe lifted his hand and examined it closely.

His first impression had been correct, he realized. Impossible as it was to believe, a chunk of the kidnapper's face had come off in his hand!

Chapter

2

"WHAT'S THAT?" Frank stared in horror at the strip of flesh his brother was holding.

"I—I think it's the kidnapper's face," Joe stammered.

"What?" Frank grabbed the shred of skin from Joe and examined it. "It's some kind of superthin rubber," he said. "Those guys were wearing masks."

"We'll worry about that later," Fenton Hardy interrupted, pushing the elevator button. "Right now, we need to call Security."

"I've already called them—*and* the police." One of the seminar participants joined the Hardys. Frank recognized him as the man who had been talking to Fenton a short time before. "I'm Paul Lindquist, head of public relations for Evanco," he said to the brothers. "Thanks, boys, for trying to help."

"Look!" a woman's voice cried from the crowd gathering around the Hardys. "They didn't go down—they're on the one hundred twenty-first floor!" Frank turned to see Paulette staring at the digital floor indicator above the elevator.

"But this building is only one hundred twenty stories high," Joe said.

"That's the maintenance floor," Mr. Lindquist told them. "There are stairs leading from there to the roof."

"Where are the other elevators?" Joe cried, pounding impatiently on the button.

"The kidnappers must have disabled them. Come on." Frank headed for a door near the elevators. "Let's take the stairs."

Fenton Hardy ran after his sons. "Paul, tell Security where we are," he called over his shoulder. "And make sure the other guests stay down here!"

Frank raced up the dimly lit stairwell ahead of Joe and his father, his heart pounding as he thought of the kidnappers escaping with Sarah Evans. He reached the top of the stairs, opened the door to the maintenance floor, then waited in the narrow corridor for the others to catch up. The corridor was lined with steel doors. Frank guessed they led to storage rooms.

"They wouldn't stay here," Joe decided, trying the first door and finding it locked. "They'd be too easy to find."

"Look." Mr. Hardy pointed to a door at the

end of the hall. A sign beside the door read Systems Operations Center. The door had been left partly ajar.

"That's it," Joe said. "Let's go."

The three Hardys raced down the corridor toward the door. Frank led the way through it and up another, narrower flight of stairs. At the top, Frank found another metal door, also left open. Boy, he thought, they didn't even bother to hide their tracks. Cautiously he opened the door wide enough to slip through. Joe and Mr. Hardy followed.

"Wow," Frank murmured as the three of them stared at the enormous room they'd entered. It was windowless, and its walls were made of metal. Frank heard the wind whistling around the outside corners and realized that they were in a room built on the skyscraper's roof. Along the walls were banks of humming computer equipment. Closed-circuit television monitors were set up in a console in the center of the room. The setup looked to Frank like a miniature version of NASA's command center.

The three Hardys turned when they heard a grunting sound behind them. A dark-skinned man with a shaved head was tied to a chair in the far corner of the room. Although he was gagged, he had been able to make enough noise to get the Hardys' attention.

"Well, they've been here," Joe remarked as they all rushed to release the man. Joe ripped a strip of tape off the man's mouth, causing him to yelp.

"Sorry," Joe said. "But did you see—"

"Of course I saw them," the man replied. "Get these ropes off. Hurry! There's a razor knife on the console."

While Joe ran to retrieve the knife, Mr. Hardy asked the man, "Who are you, anyway?"

"Kareem Addar. We'll have tea together later," the man snapped rudely. "Come on, cut the ropes!"

Joe sliced through the ropes. The moment they fell away Addar jumped from the chair and stared at one of the video monitors. Following his gaze, Frank saw an image of a helicopter with its rotors spinning. The man with the eye-patch was shoving a struggling Sarah through the open helicopter door.

"Where's the other guy?" Frank asked, staring at the image.

"No time to ask now!" Addar ran to a heavy fire door at one end of the room. "Let's stop them!"

The Hardys followed just as two men in Evanco security uniforms, their pistols drawn, burst into the room from the stairway. "We saw what was happening on the monitors downstairs," one guard said quickly. "But we couldn't get up here until we got the elevators working."

"Let's go!" Frank called to them as Addar yanked the fire door open. A freezing wind blew inside, pushing Frank back a step. He regained his footing and charged after Addar, followed by Mr. Hardy, Joe, and the security men.

Outside, the wind nearly blew Frank backward again. A helicopter landing pad, outlined by lights, took up most of the roof. Satellite dishes, microwave relays, electrical generators, and other heavy equipment surrounded it.

Frank squinted against the wind to look at the four-seater helicopter just now rising up from the pad. In the evening light, he could make out Sarah in the front passenger seat. She seemed to be struggling against the pilot's grip. Another man in the backseat leaned toward the open hatch, peering down at the Hardys.

"We're too late!" Frank heard one of the security guards shout. "They have her!"

But Joe was not about to give up. He raced toward the helipad and grabbed hold of the helicopter doorframe as it lifted away from the roof.

"Joe! Get down!" Fenton Hardy shouted.

But Joe hung on. Frank watched his brother pull himself up to the chopper's open hatch.

"Is he crazy?" the guard yelled as the group on the roof watched the helicopter move over their heads. "He'll get killed!"

Frank clenched his fists as he watched Joe struggling to enter the helicopter. Frank saw the man in the backseat wave something at Joe.

Suddenly Kareem Addar's voice cut through the noise of the chopper. "It's a gun! They're going to shoot him!"

"Hit the ground!" The shout drifted to Joe from the roof below. For a second he glanced down and saw the security guards and Kareem take refuge behind the equipment surrounding the helipad. He saw that his brother and father

15

remained standing, their eyes riveted on him. Then he turned his head—and found himself facing the muzzle of a 9-mm Beretta.

"Let go now, kid," growled the man in the chopper's backseat, "or drop one hundred twenty stories." Joe looked down. What the kidnapper said was true. The helicopter was nearing the edge of the roof, and the view past the edge made Joe's stomach turn. His gaze swung to Sarah, who stared back, wide-eyed, her mouth covered by the pilot's hand. Go, her look seemed to say. Joe realized that there was nothing he could do but obey.

Joe looked down. The helicopter was almost at the edge of the roof now. And with the wind blowing so hard, there was the possibility that he would be carried off the edge once he let go. But that was the chance he would have to take.

With one last look at the muzzle of the kidnapper's gun, Joe took a deep breath. Then he let go of the hatch and plunged through the air.

Chapter

3

A LONG MOMENT later, Joe landed on the roof of the computer room. For a minute he remained motionless on the icy surface. Six more feet to the left, he realized, and he would have missed the building altogether.

"Joe!" The wind carried Fenton Hardy's voice to his son. Joe looked down to see his father, Frank, and the two security guards staring at him from the edge of the landing pad. Joe's father looked badly shaken.

"I'm okay," Joe said, getting to his feet. "Just a little wobbly, that's all."

"You could have been killed!" Mr. Hardy said as Joe swung over the side of the control-center roof and dropped down.

It was a relief to return to the warm computer room with its gently whirring equipment. Joe sank into a chair at one of the consoles and almost immediately felt his anger return. The kidnappers had gotten away! There was no telling where they would take Sarah Evans now.

"We'll call the airport," one of the guards said. "They may be able to track those guys on radar."

"Forget about it," Kareem said. He gestured wearily toward a telephone whose wires hung loosely to the floor. "Those creeps ripped it out of the wall. You'll have to go downstairs."

The two guards started for the door to the stairway. "You guys wait till we get back," the second guard said to the Hardys. "The police will want a full report."

The Hardys nodded and the guards left. Joe watched Kareem move through the room, checking pieces of equipment.

"What *is* this place, anyway?" Joe asked him.

Kareem glared at Joe. "This *place,* as you call it, houses nearly a hundred million dollars' worth of state-of-the-art supercomputers and high-speed data transmission equipment."

"But what's it for?" Frank echoed from his own chair a few feet from Joe's.

"EXacT, of course." Addar stared at Frank incredulously. "Maybe you've heard of it. It's soon to be the best-known computer network on the planet."

"*This* is control central for EXacT?" Frank said.

Joe noted Frank's amazed expression. "What's so special about EXacT?" Joe asked.

"There's not much special about it now," Addar told him. "We're linked to only a few places so far—science labs, military research installations, universities, communication companies—in a pilot program. But when we go fully on-line, this network is going to change the world."

"How's that?" Fenton asked.

Frank exchanged a knowledgeable glance with Kareem. "I've read about it in my computer magazines," Frank said. "Basically, EXacT solves the biggest problem with computers—transferring information from one kind of computer to another. There are too many different computers in the world, using too many different kinds of software. EXacT is an interpreter—and a smart one."

Kareem nodded proudly. "With EXacT, you can use any computer, anywhere, just by hooking your own terminal up to the telephone."

"Isn't the roof kind of an unsafe place to put such a miracle?" Joe asked skeptically.

"It's the best place," Frank answered for the technician. "On a building this tall, there's practically no interference. They have their satellite links up here and everything." He turned to Addar. "Do you just work here, or did you help design this center?"

Kareem shook his head. "I wish I'd designed it. I did my thesis at M.I.T. on global interfacing. Evanco hired me after I graduated, and I've been helping get the network fully on-line ever since."

"All by yourself?" Joe asked, bewildered.

Kareem laughed. "Usually there are three or four other technicians up here with me, but the others went downstairs a few hours ago to check out who was at the reception."

Joe was about to ask Kareem about the new computer virus Frank had described earlier when the technician turned to Joe instead. "Now you can answer my questions," he said. "Who were those guys in that chopper? I was just minding my own business when they burst through the door and tied me up. What were they doing with that girl?"

"The girl is Sarah Evans," Fenton Hardy told him, "the daughter of the owner of Evanco. She was kidnapped from the reception." He shook his head. "I still don't understand why the kidnappers decided to snatch her from such a well-protected situation. It's a miracle they got away at all."

"But snatching her from the reception might have been the easiest way, if it was an inside job," Joe suggested. "Maybe the kidnappers were able to blend in with the others until they made their move."

"Mr. Hardy?" The two security guards reappeared at the top of the stairs. "The police are here. You and your sons are wanted at headquarters for questioning."

"Let's go over this again," the short, tense police officer said to Frank two hours later at the downtown Chicago precinct's headquarters.

Frank sighed. He had already told Lieutenant Gabriella Babain all he knew about the kidnapping the first time she'd questioned the Hardys. Then she insisted on cross-examining Frank and Joe again—separately this time. Mr. Hardy was allowed to remain, though. He had sat through Joe's cross-examination and was now with Frank.

"You say you'd never met Sarah Evans before this evening," the lieutenant said, pacing the tiny room. "And yet when two armed men tried to snatch her from the reception room, you were willing to tackle them in order to save her."

"At the reception only *one* man pulled a gun," Frank corrected her, "and Joe and I thought that, between the two of us, we could handle the situation. Joe and I would try to save *anyone* in trouble." He looked at his watch. It was almost ten P.M., and he was getting impatient. He glanced at the second officer, Chuck Adler, who sat typing Frank's answers on a computer at a desk in the corner.

"It seems to me," Frank continued, "that the important thing isn't why we did what we did, but how the kidnappers knew they could enter the building through the EXacT control center. EXacT's central location isn't exactly public knowledge."

"Of course—I was just about to say that," Babain snapped.

Frank exchanged a glance with his father. Mr. Hardy cleared his throat and said, "Excuse me, Lieutenant. Has the FBI been called in yet?"

"Certainly!" Babain replied. "The chopper crossed the state line into Indiana, making this a federal case. The FBI is trying to track down the kidnappers there while we do the groundwork—going over the crime scene and interviewing witnesses like yourselves. Now, do you mind if we continue?"

Frank felt annoyed to be stuck there when he and his brother could be investigating Sarah's kidnapping. And if he felt annoyed, he could only imagine how restless Joe must be by now.

Maybe I can speed things up a little, Frank decided. He reached into his pocket for the piece of rubber that Joe had pulled off the kidnapper's face. He tore off a corner for himself, then held the larger piece out for the police officer to see. "I just remembered, Lieutenant," he said. "When my brother and I were fighting the kidnappers, Joe pulled this off one of their faces. Apparently, they were wearing masks."

"Why didn't you show me this before?" Lieutenant Babain took the bit of rubber and held it up to the light.

"To tell you the truth, we were pretty surprised by the whole scene," Frank tried to explain. "It's not every day you see one of the richest girls in America kidnapped before your eyes." He ran a hand through his hair. "Any fingerprints would have been ruined in the fighting, but maybe your lab can figure out where the masks were bought."

"I know how to do my job," Babain said sharply, heading for the door with the shred of rubber. "I also know how to charge a witness with withholding evidence."

At the doorway she turned back to Frank and his father. "Wait outside while I take this to the lab. Adler, come with me."

The other officer stood and joined the lieutenant. As they marched off, Frank and his father joined a very bored-looking Joe out in the hall. "What's going on?" Joe asked as Frank dropped into a chair beside him.

"Everyone's running scared," Frank told him. "They're terrified the mayor will fire the whole precinct if they don't find Sarah by midnight."

"They're worried about their jobs?" Joe said in disgust. "What about Sarah? Has anyone mentioned a ransom note yet?"

"Not here," Mr. Hardy said. "But the FBI's involved now. I may be able to get more information from my friends there. I'll go make some calls."

After Mr. Hardy left, Joe sighed and glanced down the corridor toward the precinct's front desk. "Look who else was brought in for questioning," he remarked. Frank turned to see Kareem Addar being escorted past the desk by a police officer.

"I'm glad," Joe said. "I don't know about you, but I don't trust Kareem. He let the kidnappers inside, right? Why wasn't the outside door to the control center locked?"

"I don't know," Frank replied. "One thing I'm sure of, though. Kareem would never have let anyone touch his equipment—not even his phone—if he could help it. Besides, what reason could he have to help get Sarah Evans kidnapped?"

"Money, of course," Joe pointed out. "Let's walk down to the desk and see who else the police picked up."

The Hardys ambled down to the precinct's crowded waiting room. Frank spotted their father near the pay phones in the back, talking with a short, older man in an expensive, well-tailored suit.

Mr. Hardy waved them over. "Frank and Joe," he said when they had joined him, "this is Mr. Bruno Laird, J. P. Evans's chief-of-staff. Bruno, these are my sons."

"Ah, yes," the man boomed in a voice that seemed too loud for his size. He shook hands energetically with each boy. "I heard all about your adventures this evening from the police. You did a brave thing, trying to save our Sarah. I'm only sorry you didn't manage to succeed."

"We haven't given up yet, sir," Frank pointed out. "We have a few clues to follow up on."

Laird blinked in surprise. "Surely you've done enough already," he said, tugging on one earlobe. "We have the police on the case now."

"Don't worry, Mr. Laird," Fenton Hardy broke in gently. "My boys have worked on a number of cases already. They know how to keep from interfering in an official investigation."

"Good," Laird said.

"There's Paulette, Sarah's friend," Joe said, gazing past Laird's shoulder. He glanced at the executive. "Mind if we talk to her?" he asked.

"By all means," Laird said.

Frank noted how pale and exhausted Paulette looked.

"Hi," Paulette said to Frank and Joe as they approached. "I've been here almost two hours already, and I haven't heard any news of Sarah. How about you?"

"Nothing," Joe replied.

Paulette sighed and sat on one of the wooden chairs in the waiting room. "I've spent the entire time in one of the interrogation rooms, waiting to be questioned," she said. "Some female lieutenant was supposed to cross-examine me, but apparently she got hung up questioning someone else."

"That someone was us," Joe told her grimly. "Lieutenant Babain is so nervous she's treating even the witnesses like probable suspects."

"It's all my fault," Paulette murmured in a voice so low that the Hardys had trouble hearing her. "I'm the one who talked Sarah into going to that reception. She'd told me so much about her father's company, I wanted to see it from the inside. And now look what's happened."

"What school do you two go to?" Frank asked, hoping to distract Paulette.

"Illinois Independent University," she replied. " 'Double I,' we call it. Sarah and I were assigned as roommates our freshman year. That was three years ago, and we've been best friends ever since."

"And she never gave you a tour of Evanco before?" Joe asked, surprised.

"Actually, it was a major effort for her to take me there tonight," Paulette admitted. "To tell you the truth, Sarah hates Evanco and everything it stands for. She thinks her father made his company grow at the expense of his weaker competitors. She also believes that computer software should be made available, free, to nonprofit organizations—and Evanco is founded on the profits J.P. made selling his software for as much money as possible. Sarah and her father haven't spoken to each other in two years."

Frank and Joe exchanged a startled glance. "But she meant to talk to him tonight?" Frank asked.

Paulette nodded, close to tears. "I talked her into it. Anyway, she really misses her father. I told her the reception was a perfect way to break through J.P.'s defenses—a way of showing him she was interested in his work, even if she still had disagreements with him."

"She really misses him," Frank asked hesitantly, "or does she just miss his money?"

Paulette stiffened. "Money doesn't mean much to Sarah," she said curtly. "Her tuition and basic living expenses are paid from a trust fund in her name. I don't see what J.P.'s wealth has to do with this."

Frank didn't tell Paulette that he was wondering whether Sarah might have arranged for her own kidnapping. To a reckless girl who despised her rich father, a fake kidnapping might seem like a brilliant plan for getting her hands on what she felt was her share of the family money.

His thoughts were interrupted by the sight of Lieutenant Babain striding angrily toward them, trailed by Officer Adler. "Did I tell you boys you could talk to the other witnesses?" the lieutenant snapped.

"It's okay, ma'am," Paulette said timidly. "We were just talking about Sarah, that's all."

Lieutenant Babain threw up her hands in disgust. "Come along, then, all three of you," she said, turning back toward the interrogation rooms. She signaled to Mr. Hardy, who was still talking to Mr. Laird, that the boys would be back in a moment. "I have witness statements for you boys to sign. Since you've already chatted up Ms. Cameron here, you might as well sign them while I question her."

Frank, Joe, and Paulette followed the two officers to a small room down the hall from the one in which Frank had been questioned. Paulette and the Hardys sat around a table in the center of the room. A computer like the one Officer Adler had been using sat on a desk in the corner. It was turned on, but the screen was blank.

"Boys—your statements to sign," the lieutenant said briskly, passing a computer printout to each brother.

As the boys read their statements, the lieutenant turned to Paulette Cameron. Frank looked up and saw the dark-haired computer student shiver.

"Now for you," the policewoman began. "First, I want to know how you got into this reception, when as far as we know you weren't on any guest—''

Lieutenant Babain was interrupted by an odd humming noise. Her voice faltered as her eyes darted around the small room, trying to locate its source.

''What's that?'' Joe looked up from his reading. Even Adler, who had been loading the computer's printer with fresh paper, paused to listen.

''It sounds like a mosquito,'' Frank said as the humming noise grew louder. ''But it seems to be coming from the—''

Frank stopped talking as he looked at the computer. The noise was getting louder—more like an alarm now than a hum. And it seemed to be coming from the computer terminal itself.

Suddenly Paulette leapt to her feet. ''Get out!'' she screamed. ''Move—now!''

''What's going on?'' Frank shouted above the noise. Paulette's wild expression convinced them that she knew something they didn't.

''The computer!'' she yelled, shoving Lieutenant Babain toward the doorway. The alarm sound had by now grown to foghorn level. ''It's going to explode any second!''

Frank started toward the door, then spun around and stared at the computer. The screen was now filled with bright white light, and sparks flew across its surface. Frank stared, fascinated, as the sound increased to an ear-splitting level.

''Get out!'' Paulette screamed. Then the desktop computer exploded.

Chapter

4

"ARE YOU okay, Joe?"

At the sound of Frank's voice beside him, Joe raised his head from the floor. The force of the explosion had knocked both him and Frank to the floor. The officers and Paulette were also on the floor, having dropped instinctively when the computer exploded.

Joe stared around, bewildered. The desk in the corner of the room was smoking, and the computer that had rested on it was obliterated. Shards of glass, metal, and burnt plastic lay all around the room. A fire alarm was blaring, and the hall had filled with police straining to see in. Joe sat up and rubbed his neck. His ears were ringing and his head ached. "I can't believe the computer actually exploded."

"I know," Frank said, getting up, then helping Officer Adler to his feet. "It was unbelievable! That must be the computer virus Dad was telling us about."

"Frank! Joe! Are you all right?" Fenton Hardy called, forcefully pushing his way through the crowd. When he saw Frank and Joe staring back at him, he relaxed a little.

"What happened here?" their father asked, glancing from the boys to the room.

"The computer virus." Frank reached down to help Paulette up as well. The dark-haired girl looked stunned and frightened, but Frank saw that aside from a few scratches on her face she had suffered little harm. "You should have seen it, Dad. There was this incredible sound for about forty-five seconds, and then the computer just blew!"

"How can that happen?" Lieutenant Babain asked, stepping back as several other police officers entered to inspect the damage. The lieutenant ushered the Hardys and Paulette into an empty room across the hall. "I've never seen a machine explode before."

"It had to have been a computer virus," Mr. Hardy said. "The virus causes the power transformer to overload," he explained soberly as the shaken victims took their seats. "It's a good thing no one was sitting directly in front of that machine when it blew."

"Yes, but I want to know exactly how it exploded," Lieutenant Babain said angrily. "Who put this so-called virus into a Chicago police precinct's computer?"

"Anyone could have done it, I guess," Frank said. "Are you on the EXacT network?"

The lieutenant turned to Officer Adler. "I just type in witness reports, Lieutenant," Adler said. "I don't know anything about computers."

"If you are logged on," Mr. Hardy said, "that could explain the explosion. EXacT has been having problems with explosions lately—the computer experts call them screamers. They could be random accidents, but Evanco's troubleshooters are beginning to suspect a virus. And a virus is untraceable—it could have been picked up from a network like EXacT at any time."

"We'll check up on that," Lieutenant Babain said, scribbling a few notes on a pad. Then she turned to Officer Adler. "Adler, please check the other room and see if the statements for the Hardys are still intact. If not, then print out their statements again."

As Officer Adler left the room, the lieutenant said to Frank and Joe, "Gentlemen, once you've signed the statements, you may leave, and I'll begin questioning Ms. Cameron."

"You're still going to question me?" Paulette protested. "Hasn't enough happened today?"

"You want to help your friend, don't you?" the lieutenant prodded.

"Of course I do." Paulette glowered at the officer. "But from what I've seen, talking to you isn't going to help Sarah one bit. Then, in a voice so low only Frank and Joe managed to hear, she added, "I have my own way of getting back at the enemy."

"What was that supposed to mean?" Joe asked his brother a few minutes later as they left police headquarters with their father. By then the chaos in the corridors had subsided. An arson crew was already at work in the ruined interrogation room, and all visitors, including the reporters interviewing police about the kidnapping, had been herded back to the waiting area. As the Hardys stepped out onto the chilly city sidewalk, Joe was relieved to realize that the ringing sound in his ears was nearly gone.

"You mean what Paulette said about getting back at the enemy?" Frank asked him. "Your guess is as good as mine."

"I'm starting to wonder if Paulette knows more about this kidnapping than she's letting on," Joe said. "Let's try to talk to her again tomorrow."

"You'll do nothing of the kind," Mr. Hardy said sternly as he waved down a cab. "That explosion tonight may or may not have been a coincidence. In any event, this case is getting far too dangerous."

The boys started to object, but their father firmly ushered them into the cab. "No arguments," he announced as he joined them in the backseat. "Starting tomorrow, we concentrate on what we came here for—to share information on computer security. I'll stay in touch with my contacts at the FBI and keep you posted on their progress. But otherwise, getting summer jobs is your number-one priority. Is that understood?"

"Sure, Dad." Joe exchanged a guilty look with his brother. Now, he realized, the two of them would not only have to do their sleuthing behind Lieutenant Babain's back, they'd have to hide it from their own father, too.

For a moment, when Joe woke the next morning between fresh-smelling sheets in his and Frank's room at the Fairmont Hotel, he almost believed the events of the night before had occurred in a terrible dream. Still lying in bed, he reached for the phone, relishing the thought of a big room-service breakfast.

"It's about time you woke up." The note of excitement in Frank's voice dispelled any hope that the kidnapping hadn't occurred. "Welcome to Chicago's biggest news story of the year. We made the papers. And if you sit up quick, you might catch a glimpse of yourself on TV."

With a sigh, Joe pulled himself to a sitting position. Why was he so sore, he wondered? Oh, yes—now he remembered—fighting with the kidnapper, hanging on to a flying helicopter, being knocked down by an exploding computer. And he'd thought a computer seminar would be boring!

Frank was already dressed and sitting on the foot of his bed, watching a television report of the kidnapping. He had the volume turned down low. Joe blinked sleepily as images of the Evanco

Building, the reception room, and several executives flashed on the screen.

"Who's that?" Joe asked. It was a photograph of a white-haired man with a short-clipped mustache and narrow, cold blue eyes.

"J. P. Evans himself," Frank answered. "Sarah has his blue eyes, but that's about all the resemblance, don't you think?"

"He looks mean," Joe said, watching with interest now.

"The newspaper reports say he's a weirdo," Frank told his brother. "According to them, he has all kinds of Howard Hughes–type hang-ups. He refuses to talk on the phone because he's terrified of germs. He wears gloves in case someone shakes his hand. He spends most of his time holed up in an isolated room someplace, and Bruno Laird carries out all his orders."

"Laird? That guy Dad introduced us to last night?" Joe asked.

"Right. No wonder Evans's daughter feels alienated from him."

Frank's face brightened. "Look," he said. "There we are."

Joe caught a glimpse of all three Hardys being ushered into a police car outside the Evanco Building. Joe laughed. "Hey, we don't look bad. I hope some Hollywood producer is watching this now."

Frank turned up the volume. "Mr. Evans was notified of Sarah's disappearance while in Sydney, Australia, addressing a convention of international businessmen," the newscaster said.

"Through Bruno Laird, the billionaire issued a statement expressing horror at the kidnapping. He is offering a reward for his daughter's return. He is currently on his way to Chicago in his private jet."

"That's strange." Joe looked at his brother. "Paulette said she and Sarah went to last night's reception especially to see Evans. Wouldn't Sarah have known if he was in Australia?"

"Maybe he meant to be back in Chicago by then but got hung up," Frank suggested. "I guess a guy who refuses to use phones and who isn't speaking to his daughter anyway might not bother to let her know he's not going to show."

Joe sighed, got out of bed, and switched off the television. "I wish we could go ahead and investigate this case," he said. "I can't believe Dad wants us to leave it to the police when Sarah's out there somewhere waiting to be rescued."

"You know, Joe," Frank said, leaning back on his elbows on the bed, "I don't think Dad believed for a minute we'd follow his advice. I think he was just giving orders so he'd be in the clear if Mom found out."

"You think so?" Joe crossed to the dresser to get some clothes. "You mean, he wants us to stay off the case, but he doesn't want us to stay off it?"

"I guess he wants us to stay off it all right, but let's face it—Dad should know we're not the types to back off when we're this close to the action."

Joe frowned. "Speaking of Dad, where is he?"

"You were sleeping so soundly, he went to the breakfast at Evanco without us," Frank replied. "So hurry up and get dressed. If we're quick, we can cram in some investigating before the morning session."

"I don't care what you have planned," Joe protested. "I'm cramming in juice and a couple of rolls first."

It was nearly nine o'clock by the time Frank and Joe hurried the few blocks from the Fairmont to the Evanco Building. "You're sure Dad won't kill us for not showing up for the first seminar session?" Joe asked his brother.

"The seminar's being held in the Evanco Building, in any case," Frank replied. "If Dad catches us there, we'll just say we got lost."

"I don't like to go behind his back like this," Joe admitted.

"Neither do I," Frank said. "But when we've solved this case, he'll be grateful."

Joe shrugged, resigned, as they entered the skyscraper's spacious lobby. Twenty-foot trees were planted in the entryway, and a waterfall cascaded down one wall. A dozen security guards stood about, carefully watching all passersby. It was obvious that security had been increased.

"Evans may be weird, but he sure knows how to decorate," Joe said, shaking his head in amazement. "Where to first? The reception room?"

"Let's try the EXacT control center," Frank suggested. The boys presented their seminar passes to a security guard behind a massive marble desk, then proceeded to the elevator bank that serviced only the top thirty floors. Pushing the elevator button, Frank added, "I want to ask Kareem, or whoever else is there, about the so-called screamer that went off at police headquarters last night. I bet they can tell us more about what's really going on with that virus than Dad will find out in an official seminar."

The first stop on the elevator was the ninetieth floor. Joe felt his stomach drop as they sped upward. After the ninetieth floor, a number of employees got on and off the elevator. But by the time the Hardys reached the top, they were alone again.

"Just one more floor," Frank said as the boys entered the long, narrow corridor on the maintenance floor and headed for the stairwell.

"Hello?" Frank called as the Hardys climbed the stairs to the control center. Joe could hear radio music playing and the low murmur of conversation. When they cleared the threshold of the large computer room, four workers in their early twenties turned to greet them.

"Hi." Joe eyed the workers. All four were casually dressed in jeans and T-shirts or sweaters. "We're, uh—"

"We know who you are," said the worker nearest the Hardys. He put down the soda can in his hand and ambled over to shake hands with the Hardys. "I'm Mike Koster. We saw you on the videotape, man."

The pony-tailed technician turned to his fellow workers. "Meet the supporting cast of today's afternoon movie!" he told them. Then he turned back to the Hardys. "Our automatic surveillance cameras caught the whole thing on video. The kidnappers breaking through the door and tying up Kareem, and then carrying Sarah out. We even caught a glimpse of you guys trying to stop the chopper. That was amazing!"

"Too bad Kareem wasn't watching the monitors before it happened," one of the other technicians said loudly over the noise of the radio. "There's tape of the guys landing and starting to break in. Kareem always did concentrate too hard on his work for his own good."

Or else he was conspiring with the kidnappers, Joe thought. In that case he would have made a point of not looking at the video. He also wondered why none of the security guards had been looking at the monitors on the main floor before the kidnappers turned off the elevators. He made a mental note to check it out later.

"We edited the whole sequence this morning," the first technician continued. "So anyway, have a seat. What can we do for you guys?"

"Well, actually," Frank said, sitting in one of the swivel chairs, "we were looking for Kareem."

"Dead asleep, I'm afraid," a third man informed them from the back of the room. "He said that the interrogation session was brutal. He didn't get home till three this morning.''

Joe glanced at his brother. It appeared that Lieutenant Babain had suspicions about Kareem, too.

"What did you want to talk to him about?" Mike asked, taking a sip of his soda. "Maybe we can help you."

Joe said over the music, "Actually, we wanted to ask Kareem about screamers."

Joe saw that his last word had an instant effect. The technicians' smiles froze on their faces, and they stared at Joe suspiciously.

"Uh—screamers?" Mike said in a choked voice. "What do you know about them?"

"Just that when they explode in police interrogation rooms they tend to cut up witnesses' faces," Frank said sharply. "We hear there's been a rash of them traveling through your network. We hoped you could tell us how extensive the damage might get."

The technicians exchanged wary glances, then looked back defiantly at the Hardys. "Pretty extensive, I guess." Mike's expression remained neutral. "If by extensive you mean they might bring about the end of the world."

"The end of the—" Joe stared at Mike in disbelief. The technician, so friendly a minute ago, now eyed him with suspicion.

"The civilized world, at least," Mike said. "The virus travels over the telephone wires and through computer modems, as far as we can tell. Every computer hooked up to a modem is in danger of exploding. Screamers could cause stock market crashes, wipe out currency exchange records, prevent the air force from flying, and shut down TV news stations. You name it, a screamer could probably shut it down."

"And then panic sets in," Joe suggested, remembering the police station the night before. "There'd probably be riots everywhere once people found out what had happened."

"You said it," Mike agreed. "Actually, it's a shame you didn't show up an hour earlier. *The* expert on the subject was right here in this room."

"The expert on screamers?" Frank asked.

"That's right." Mike turned his gaze on Frank. "Her name is Paulette Cameron."

Chapter

5

"PAULETTE!" Frank exchanged a look with his brother. "How can she be an expert on screamers?"

"She said she talked to you at the police station," Mike responded. "Didn't she tell you she's studying computer science at Double I? Evanco tried to hire her, but she decided to wait and get her degree."

Frank's troubled gaze cut to Joe again. Paulette had told them about her computer experience, but this new information revealed that nearly everything else she'd said to them had been a lie. Why would she say that Sarah had taken her to the reception to introduce her to the executives at Evanco if she'd already been offered a job? And why didn't she mention that she knew all about screamers after the computer exploded at the police precinct?

Frank was about to ask Mike why Paulette had visited the control center when the stairwell door opened and a tall, bald man in a business suit appeared. "Listen up, boys," he said as he stepped through the doorway. "I just got a call that a police lieutenant at the local precinct wants to come back up here and look at the—"

The man stopped when he saw the Hardys. "Who are you?" he demanded.

"Frank and Joe Hardy, sir," Frank said, extending his hand. The man looked at the brothers suspiciously.

"We were the ones who tried to save Sarah Evans from the kidnappers last night," Frank reminded him.

"Hardy!" The man gave a grunt of recognition. "I'm Conrad Seethus, chief of security for Evanco. My boss—Mr. Laird—is looking for you. I was going to hunt you down after I talked to these guys."

"That's okay, Seethus, we get the picture," Mike said with a wave. "The police inspectors come, we show them the videotape of the kidnapping, and they go. Of course, they'll want to know where *you* were last night when Evanco's guests were being attacked, but we'll come up with a good excuse."

"I was on my way home, wise guy," Seethus said. "When I left, at six, everything was calm."

"Oh? And where were the guards who were supposed to be watching the monitors downstairs?"

"Listen," Seethus said angrily. "I don't owe you any explanation. All my men were accounted for. The two men at the desk went up to the seventy-ninth floor to check on what turned out to be a false alarm. You want more of an explanation, go ask the police."

"Temper, temper." Mike obviously enjoyed provoking the chief of security. "Well, good luck, you guys," he added to the Hardys. "Laird's not an easy man to talk to."

"We met him at the police station last night," Joe told him. "He seemed okay."

"Oh, I'm sure at police headquarters he'd try hard to be civil," the technician said, swiveling around to face his computer screen again. "On his own turf, he eats employees for breakfast."

Frank glanced at his brother and shrugged. Civil or not, they couldn't pass up this chance to talk to the second highest executive at Evanco.

As Conrad Seethus led the Hardys to the stairs, Joe asked the technician, "Is there any chance we can see that videotape of yours?"

"Sure, it'll be here," Mike answered. "Come back any time."

On the way down in the elevator, Frank wondered why Bruno Laird wanted to talk to Joe and him. He hadn't seemed very interested in them the night before—but then, of course, he'd had a major disaster on his hands. Could Laird have come up with new information on the kidnapping that he wanted to check out with eyewitnesses?

Conrad Seethus ushered the Hardys into the ninetieth-floor executive reception area with its thick, rose-colored carpeting and expensive leather furniture.

"Mr. Seethus," a middle-aged secretary said, nodding pleasantly to the group. "I'll tell Mr. Laird you're here."

Frank was even more impressed when the chief of security led the boys into the office of Mr. Laird himself. It's three times as big as our living room back home, Frank thought. He admired the enormous mahogany desk with its own elaborate computer system, the built-in bookcases, and the complex audiovisual system against the rear wall. Glass walls offered spectacular views of the winter sun shining on Lake Michigan.

"There you are!" Laird boomed, standing up behind his desk to shake the Hardys' hands. "I had hoped Conrad would find you here. Where were they, Conrad—sniffing around the halls for clues?"

"Practically, sir," Seethus said. "Actually, I found them up in the—"

"Never mind." Laird stopped him with an impatient wave of the hand. "You're here now, aren't you, boys? Have a seat! Conrad, that will be all, thank you."

Seethus blinked several times, then turned on his heel and exited the office. Frank and Joe sank into a pair of overstuffed leather chairs facing Laird's desk. Frank glanced at his brother and could tell that Joe was wondering the same thing he was: why the royal treatment from an executive with at least one major crisis on his mind?

"Uh—I guess you're wondering why I called you here," the executive said, tugging nervously at his earlobe. "Can I get you anything? A soft drink?"

"Nothing, thank you, sir," Frank said firmly, just wanting the man to get to the point.

"Yes, of course. Well." Abruptly Laird sat down behind his desk. Leaning toward the Hardys, he said in a low voice, "You see, boys, these police interrogations about who might have held a grudge against Sarah Evans or her father—my boss—started me thinking. Last night I was sure a terrorist group of some kind must have snatched Sarah. Someone with a grudge against Evanco might stoop to snatching the owner's daughter in exchange for a promise of money or a change in a company policy."

Frank nodded, wondering whether the executive's obvious nervousness could be explained by the fact that his boss must be going crazy with worry by now.

"But when we hadn't received a ransom note by this morning," Laird continued, "I guessed there must be some other motive for the crime." He peered across his desk at the Hardys. "Revenge, perhaps."

"Revenge?" Joe asked. "Who wants revenge against Evans?"

"Plenty of people," Laird said, and gave a brief laugh. He leaned back in his chair, looking thoughtful. "There's one man in particular I have in mind, though. His name is Taylor Hayes. Evans fired him a short while ago. I thought of him because he left under rather ugly circumstances, making a lot of fuss, threatening to sue the corporation, and so on.'

"And you think he was angry enough to kidnap Sarah?" Frank asked.

"I'm just thinking out loud, you understand," Laird replied. "But certainly a man with that sort of history should be investigated."

"What sort of work did he do here?" Joe asked.

"He was J.P.'s closest confidant, until he was fired," Laird informed them. "A brilliant scientist as well as Mr. Evans's personal friend. In fact, he acted as a kind of liaison between J.P. and Sarah after they stopped speaking to each other. He relayed messages and birthday presents and handled Sarah's trust fund. Now I handle those duties. But the point, you see, is that Hayes already knew Sarah quite well."

"Have you talked to the police about this?" Frank asked.

"I just thought of Hayes this morning," Laird admitted. "I don't have any concrete evidence."

"Then why tell us?" Joe asked.

"Because you're here," he answered simply. "Knowing what I do about you two, you're not going to sit by and let this case get away. I figure you might as well be doing something constructive while you're snooping around."

Frank frowned. The connection between Hayes and the kidnapping was too weak to take very seriously. And Laird's eagerness to share his suspicions with the boys made Frank wonder what Laird's own intentions were.

"Could you give us Mr. Hayes's address?" Joe asked.

"Oh, no. That I couldn't do." Laird frowned at Joe. "It's company policy never to give out personal information. Besides, I wouldn't want an accusation to be traced back to me. This kind of investigation has to be carried out very quietly, you understand. It's for the sake of the company—and Mr. Evans."

Before Joe could reply, a buzzer sounded on the desk. Laird picked up the phone receiver, listened for a moment, then hung up without speaking. "Excuse me for a moment," he said, getting up from his desk. "I'll be right back."

When they were alone in the office, Joe looked at Frank and asked, "Do you get the feeling you're being used?"

"Why—because Laird could barely stand to have us near the case last night, and this morning he's handing us suspects on a silver platter?" Frank asked. He got to his feet. "I say we check out his Rolodex."

As Joe watched, Frank headed straight for the file of small index cards he'd seen on the top of Laird's desk. Each card contained a name and address. Frank flipped through quickly to the letter *H*.

"Hurry up," Joe said. "He said he'd be right back."

"Here it is. Hayes." Frank rummaged in his pockets. "Do you have a pen?" he asked Joe.

"No," Joe said. "Hurry!"

Frank yanked open Laird's desk drawer and pulled out a pen and paper. Leaving the drawer open, he wrote down Hayes's address and phone number. "Okay," he said, shoving the pen and paper back in the drawer and sticking the paper in his pocket. "See? I told you it was—"

Frank stopped in the middle of his sentence. The door to the office had opened, and Bruno Laird stood watching him.

Chapter

6

"WHY ARE YOU going through my desk?" Bruno Laird asked Frank.

"I—I wanted to borrow a pen," Frank stammered.

"I see. And what did you want the pen for?" Laird strode into the office and swept Frank out of his way. He opened his desk drawer wide and inspected the contents.

"Look, Mr. Laird, we were just copying down Hayes's address," Joe protested, defending his brother. "You wanted us to have it, right? You just didn't want to give it to us. It's not such a big deal."

"Oh, but it *is* a big deal." Laird shut the drawer with a tiny click. "It's a matter of trust, boys. I trust you to carry out an investigation along the proper lines, and you trust me not to get in your way. I trust you to supply me with any information you unearth, and you trust me not to report you to Security for going through my desk."

"But, Mr. Laird!" Frank cried. "I was just—"

"That's enough." Laird sat down at his desk and began scribbling on a pad of paper. After a moment he looked up as though surprised to see that the boys were still there. "You may go," he said. "But report back to me on what you find."

"No wonder he's Evans's right-hand man," Joe muttered as he and his brother got on the elevator. "Talk about eccentric!"

"At least we have a good excuse for having missed the first session of the seminar," Frank said grimly. "And Laird's wanting us to investigate the case is a perfect argument for Dad."

"That's lucky," Joe said as the elevator doors opened to the downstairs lobby. "Because there's Dad now, and he doesn't look happy."

"Boys!" Mr. Hardy called as Frank and Joe stepped out of the elevator. "Where have you been?"

"Sorry, Dad," Frank said, joining his father. "Mr. Laird asked to talk to us. He wants us to investigate the kidnapping—in a hush-hush way, of course."

"Bruno Laird wants *you* to investigate?" Mr. Hardy looked from Frank to Joe. "What got into him?" he asked, half to himself.

"He suspects a guy named Taylor Hayes who

used to work here," Joe explained. "We're going to check him out. Did you talk to your friends at the FBI?"

"That's why I was looking for you," Mr. Hardy said. "I made another call five minutes ago. Apparently, there have been a huge number of crank calls on this case, but that's typical when the victim's father is as well known as J. P. Evans. The only solid news is that the helicopter the kidnappers used was discovered in an Indiana field. The pilot was inside, gagged and bound."

"The pilot?" Joe said, remembering the man with the eyepatch behind the controls of the chopper. "What's his name?"

His father took a small notebook from his pocket and checked his notes. "Sangmin Lee. He runs a helicopter charter service out of O'Hare Airport, transporting personnel for corporations. He claims that two men walked up to him on the landing field yesterday evening while he was going through a preflight check. They forced him at gunpoint to fly them to the roof of this building. Then they tied him up, put him in the backseat, and left for fifteen minutes. When they returned they had Sarah with them. They kept him tied up in back and flew the chopper away themselves."

"Then what happened?" asked Frank.

"They landed in the field and left the pilot there. He was just found," Fenton said, replacing the notebook in his pocket. "He said the girl was giving her kidnappers a hard time."

"That's good to hear." Frank turned to see Paulette Cameron standing behind the group, her eyes flashing at what Mr. Hardy had said. "Sarah's our best hope, if you ask me," she told the Hardys. "She'll probably kick and scratch her way free before we can figure out where she is."

"What are you doing here?" Joe asked. "You forgot to tell the technicians upstairs about last night's screamer?"

Paulette turned pale. "I—you talked to the guys in the control room?"

"We sure did," Frank said, taking her firmly by the arm. "Dad, do you mind if we take Paulette to lunch? We should be able to finish with the work Laird gave us by late this afternoon."

Mr. Hardy sighed. "All right, boys," he said. "I'll take notes on today's talks in case there's anything that might interest you. But there's nothing I can do about those summer jobs." He turned and walked toward the elevators.

Immediately Frank steered Paulette toward the exit doors, with Joe right behind them.

"Where are we going?" Paulette protested.

"First, we're going to eat lunch," Frank said, his jaw set in anger. "Then, we're going to ask you a few questions—like, why you told us you were meeting Mr. Evans last night when, as it turns out, he was in Australia. And why you didn't mention you're an expert on screamers."

"And why you said you wanted to meet Evanco's top executives when they'd already offered you a job," Joe added as they passed through the revolving doors.

Outside, Paulette hesitated. "Okay. I know I haven't been completely honest with you guys—"

"You've lied from the beginning," Joe said.

"I have my reasons," Paulette insisted. "I wasn't sure I could trust you before."

Frank glanced behind her at several reporters loitering outside the building, trying to interview Evanco employees about the kidnapping case. "Either you trust us, Paulette, or we skip lunch and go straight to the police," he told the girl.

"Look," Paulette said nervously, "there *is* something I want to show you. It's in Sarah's and my dorm room at Double I. Would you mind driving over there with me? I think it might help you figure out this case. Then we can eat lunch at a restaurant near the campus."

Frank glanced at Joe. He knew they didn't have much choice. Paulette was the best source for information they had so far. Frank decided they'd play it her way. "Where's your car?" he asked.

By the time the Hardys and Paulette arrived on the campus of Illinois Independent University, Paulette had explained to the boys that her job offer from Evanco had been a secret—especially from J. P. Evans's daughter. "Sarah would have murdered me if she even suspected I had dealings with Evanco," Paulette informed them. "She really hates that company—and hated it even more back then. It's only because her father's getting old that she agreed to talk to him at all. Obviously," she added, "I couldn't tell you I'd had a job offer if I hadn't told my best friend.''

Frank gazed out the car window at the university's snow-covered lawns. The campus was nearly deserted now during the winter break. ''But why did you tell us you went to the reception to further your career?'' he asked.

''Because I couldn't tell you about Sarah's and J.P.'s reconciliation,'' Paulette said impatiently, parking her car in the nearly vacant lot in front of an attractive modern dormitory. ''Sarah made me swear not to tell anyone. She didn't want stories about it leaking to the press. I mean—what if it didn't work out? When you're as rich as Sarah is, you have to worry about those things.''

''Okay,'' Joe said wearily as they climbed out of the car. ''Then tell us why you went to the party even though J.P. wasn't going to be there.''

''We didn't know J.P. wouldn't be there,'' Paulette insisted. She turned to face Joe, her green eyes flashing. ''In fact, that's what I want to tell you about. I think J.P. lured Sarah to the reception.''

''*Lured* her?'' Frank repeated. ''Why?''

Paulette led the boys inside the lobby of the dorm and down the first-floor corridor. ''Because,'' she said, her voice echoing in the deserted hallway, ''J.P. wanted to kidnap his daughter.''

They had come to a stop in front of one of the doors. ''J. P. Evans kidnapped his own daughter?'' Frank hooted. ''That's ridiculous! What for?''

''There's more to this case than you realize, Frank Hardy.'' Paulette's eyes rose to meet his. ''I'll explain later. But first,'' she added, her gaze faltering, ''I want to point out that when I left here this morning, I locked this door.''

Frank and Joe stared at the door. It stood slightly ajar. Frank slowly eased the door open and carefully stuck his head inside. ''No one's here,'' Frank said.

Paulette and Joe followed him into the room. ''Oh, no!'' Paulette exclaimed. ''Someone was here, all right. They trashed the place.''

''This isn't how you usually keep it, you mean?'' Joe quipped as he and Frank picked their way through tossed dresser drawers, clothes, books, and papers to the center of the room. ''Why do you think someone would do this?''

''I guess it has something to do with Sarah,'' Paulette answered. The window was open, and she walked over and closed it, then turned.

''I'm calling the police.'' Frank reached for the phone on a table between the pair of twin beds.

''Don't do that!'' Paulette cried. ''I mean, it doesn't look like they took anything. The TV's still here, and the computer. I'll just report it to campus security when we—''

''Forget it, Paulette,'' Frank said, dialing the operator. ''We've listened to your stories long enough. It's time the police got involved.''

Joe watched Paulette as, furious, she turned her back on Frank and began picking up papers and piling them on one of the two desks in the room. "It's not as though I can't take care of this," she protested in a low voice to Joe as Frank talked over the phone to the receptionist at police headquarters. "If I'd wanted the police to be involved, I would have called them myself."

"You said you had something to show us," Joe reminded her coldly.

Paulette turned her gaze on him. "I did," she admitted. "And when you see them, maybe you'll start believing me."

As Frank hung up the phone, Paulette hurried to one of a pair of chests of drawers. Most of the drawers had been pulled out, their contents tossed about the room. But Paulette reached underneath the paper lining of one of the bottom drawers and took out a number of letters.

"Sarah kept these here," she told Joe, holding the letters out to him. "She told me to read them in case anything ever happened to her. She said they'd tell me who had done her harm. I read them a long time ago, of course, in secret," she added, sitting down at the foot of one of the beds. "They're from her father. He threatens her in every one of them."

Joe took one of the letters out of its envelope and scanned the typewritten contents while Frank read over his shoulder. "This says he'll cut off her trust fund if she doesn't stop organizing against Evanco," Joe said. He took out another one. "This one says if she doesn't stop giving reporters interviews about her robber-baron father, he'll have her tied up and locked in her room.''

"See what I mean?" Paulette said triumphantly. "Evans is a monster. He'd be happy to kidnap his own daughter if she dared get in his way.''

"But these letters are typed, so we can't identify the writer for sure," Frank pointed out. "And they're dated a year, two years ago.''

"What difference does that make?" Paulette asked angrily. "As long as I've known Sarah, her father has been nothing but cruel to her. Now he claims he wants to be friends again. I don't believe him! I think he kidnapped her and hid her away so she'd never embarrass him or Evanco again.''

In the silence that followed, Joe heard a faint hum. Turning slowly, he saw that it came from the computer on one of the desks. "Paulette, did you leave your computer on when you left this morning?''

Paulette stood up and stared at the machine. "No, I didn't," she said softly. "And the monitor's turned off. I never do that." Paulette crossed the room to the computer and switched on the monitor. Gradually light filled the small computer screen.

"It's a message," Joe said as he made out the words typed on the screen. " 'To Save Sarah, Check Comptellit,' " he read. "What does that mean?''

"Comptellit is a computer bulletin board," Frank explained. "People use it to leave electronic mail, notices—you know, messages and stuff. In this case, it looks like the kidnappers may have left their ransom note there. Not a bad idea—a bulletin board message is impossible to trace."

"Can we log onto it now?" Joe asked eagerly.

"No," Paulette told him. "My modem's at the shop, being fixed."

"We'll have to show this to the police then," Frank said. He glanced out the window. "Here they come, right on time." He picked up the stack of letters. "Wait until we give them these."

"No!" Paulette leapt for the letters and grabbed them from Frank's hand. "I told you, no police!" she said shrilly, backing toward the computer. "If you tell the cops, J.P.'s letters will be in the papers tomorrow morning, and Sarah will never speak to me again!"

"She'll never speak to you again if she stays kidnapped!" Frank shouted back. He lunged for the letters, but Paulette dodged out of his way. Quickly she switched her computer off.

"What are you doing?" Frank yelled as he watched the words on the screen fade to black. "You've destroyed vital evidence, Paulette."

"They won't believe it." Paulette glanced behind her to see whether the police had arrived. "Anyone could have put that message there. And you said yourself that anyone could have typed these letters, too. I'm depending on you, Frank and Joe. Get J.P. before he hurts Sarah. It's up to you."

"We won't protect you this time, Paulette,"

Joe said. He walked toward her slowly, holding out his hand for the letters. "Don't you see? You've told us too many lies. We don't know who to trust in this case, but we know by now we can't trust you."

Joe swallowed. He hated to betray Paulette, who was staring at him as though she couldn't believe what she had heard. But he didn't have any choice.

Suddenly Paulette shoved the letters beneath the computer and whirled around to face the door. "Officers!" Paulette screamed as the two policemen entered the room. "These boys are assaulting me! Arrest them!"

Chapter

7

"FREEZE!" The first policeman responded instantly, grabbing Joe by the arms. A moment later Joe and Frank both stood facing the wall, their arms twisted behind their backs and their wrists handcuffed.

"What happened, miss?" the second policeman asked. He was middle-aged, with a deeply lined face.

"I was walking down the hall, and I noticed the door to my room was open," Paulette said quickly, backing away from the boys. "These two guys were inside, going through my things. When I tried to stop them, they attacked me."

"That's a lie!" Frank shouted, slowly turning to face the policemen. "We came here with her. I'm the one who called you. Our names are Frank and Joe Hardy. We're in Chicago for a seminar at Evanco. We were the ones who tried to save Sarah Evans from her kidnappers—"

"Oh, yeah," the younger policeman said. "I remember seeing you two at headquarters last night." He looked at Paulette. "Weren't you there, too?"

"The point is, she has evidence in the case, and she doesn't want to give it to you," Frank said. "It's a stack of letters stuffed under the computer. They're threats from Sarah Evans's father. We thought the police should have them, and Paulette got mad."

Frank's words changed the policemen's attitude completely. While the older officer watched the Hardys, the younger man retrieved the letters from beneath the computer. Joe glanced over his shoulder to see Paulette fuming as the policeman went through the letters, scanning the contents.

"They're threats, all right," the policeman said to his partner, "addressed to 'Sarah' and signed 'Dad.' Now, young lady," he said to Paulette, "do you still want to file charges against these two?"

"N-no," Paulette stammered. "Just let them go."

"Because if you want to file charges," the policeman continued, ignoring her, "then you'll have to come down to headquarters to sign a complaint. And while you're there, I'm sure Lieutenant Babain will have a few more questions for you."

"No, really, I've changed my mind," Paulette

repeated. "Go ahead and take the letters. And you can just let these guys go."

"We can escort them outside if you want us to," the older policeman said, taking the handcuffs off Frank. The younger policeman did the same for Joe.

"Don't bother," Paulette said as Frank and Joe, released, turned to face her. "I can handle these two myself."

"Why didn't you just hand over the letters in the first place?" Frank demanded after the policemen had left. "If they'd wanted to, they could have taken us all down to police headquarters, and we'd have spent the day being questioned."

"I need those letters!" Paulette protested. "They're the only evidence I have that Sarah's father means her harm."

"We've wasted enough time here, Frank," Joe said to his brother. "I say we go back to Evanco. If this really was an inside job, we need to start running checks on any suspicious employees."

"Right," Frank said. "Let's go."

"Wait a minute!" Paulette protested. "You're acting like I'm completely out of this investigation."

Joe turned to her. "Unless you're the kidnapper, Paulette, I guess you are. We can't trust you, so we're better off investigating on our own."

"But I'm depending on you to find Sarah,"

Paulette insisted. "The police will never do it. Evans is too important in this town, and if he kidnapped his daughter, the police will look the other way."

"Come on, Paulette," Frank said. "You don't know Evans—"

"*You* don't know Evans," Paulette said, her eyes narrowing. "If you'd met him, you'd know what I mean. I'll tell you what. You haven't talked to that helicopter pilot I heard your father telling you about. Why not go to O'Hare with me tomorrow? We'll interview him together."

Frank sighed. It seemed as if they were never going to be able to get rid of Paulette, now that she'd decided the Hardys were necessary to retrieve her friend.

"Come on," she pleaded. "I'll make you a deal. Go with me tomorrow, and I'll drive you back to Evanco now. You won't have to take a cab."

"Okay," Frank said, relenting. "Tomorrow morning. Nine o'clock."

"Great!" Paulette said. "I'll drive you back now." She headed toward the door. "Oh, and, uh—sorry about almost getting you arrested," she added. "It was just the first thing that popped into my head. Amazingly enough, it almost worked!"

"She sure is weird," Frank remarked after Paulette had dropped the Hardys off in front of the Evanco Building and driven off with a friendly wave. Several reporters still stood outside the building, but again, in their search for executives to interview, none of them seemed to recognize the Hardys.

"You said it," Joe said, following his brother into the building. "But I'm too hungry to think about her. Do we finally get to eat, or are you going to make us start checking out employees right away?"

"We'll grab a sandwich at the employee cafeteria later," Frank told him. "First, though, we're paying another visit to the EXacT network's control center." Both boys flashed their ID cards to the guard behind the desk.

"What for?" Joe asked as they walked to the elevator bank.

"First, the guys at EXacT should be able to hook up with Comptellit so we can read whatever message the kidnappers left on the electronic bulletin board," Frank told him. "Second, we may be able to use the computers to go through the Evanco employees' backgrounds. And third, I hope we'll run into Kareem Addar up there. I'd like to ask him a few questions."

Even as the Hardys climbed the stairs to the control center, Joe could hear loud rock and roll music blasting on the radio. He and Frank crossed the threshold of the large room to find Kareem and two other technicians pretending to play guitars to the music while their computers whirred and blinked.

"Excuse me," Frank shouted over the noise. "Are we bothering you guys?"

Kareem stopped playing his imaginary guitar long enough to recognize the Hardys. "Hi. I see you survived Lieutenant Babain. Come on in and listen to the music."

"Actually," said Joe, walking over to the radio and turning down the volume, "we were wondering if you might be able to help us out. We understand Sarah Evans's kidnappers left a message on Comptellit's bulletin board, and we hoped you could call it up."

"They've finally made contact, huh?" Kareem said. "How'd you find out?"

"It's a long story," Frank said tersely. "What we need to do now is read the message."

Kareem exchanged a glance with his two fellow workers. "Okay, I can connect you," he said. He leaned over his computer keyboard and began typing.

A moment later, Joe saw the Comptellit logo appear on Kareem's computer screen. Several options were listed, including Games, Library References, Travel Services, and Bulletin Board.

"Bulletin board," said Kareem, punching the corresponding number on the keyboard.

Instantly the screen changed to a menu, listing the messages currently on the bulletin board by names or key words. Joe scanned the list as Kareem scrolled down with the arrow key.

"That's it," Joe said. " 'Message for the FBI.' We found it, Frank!"

Kareem selected that message and pressed the

Enter key on his keyboard. "Uh-oh," he said. "We need a password."

" 'Room Number,' " Frank read from the screen. "What room number?"

"A hotel room?" Joe asked.

Frank shook his head. "How about Paulette and Sarah's room number at the dorm?"

"Right!" Joe gave the number to Kareem, who typed it in. An instant later, a page of text appeared.

"Bingo," said Kareem as the two other technicians joined the Hardys to read the message. "Whoa, this is hot stuff!" He cleared his throat and read aloud, " 'This message goes to J. P. Evans. We know you're holding your daughter against her will. Now the FBI knows, too. Release Sarah, unharmed, or screamers will "EXacT" a heavy toll. You have twenty-four hours to comply.' "

Kareem swiveled in his chair and stared at Frank and Joe. "End of message," he announced.

Chapter

8

"PAULETTE LEFT that message," Joe insisted, staring at the computer screen. "She's the one who suspects Evans of kidnapping Sarah. She's the only person we know who could threaten to plant screamers in someone's computer system. And she led us to this message in the first place."

"She's been acting strange from the very beginning," Frank agreed. "But if she left the message for Evans, why would she have bothered pretending it was left by someone else? Besides, whoever left this message obviously wants the FBI involved, but Paulette wouldn't even let the police see the computer message."

Joe stared at the computer screen. "I guess the sender could be one of the cranks Dad was telling us about," he suggested, "but it would

have to be a crank who knew about screamers."
Joe sighed. "The deeper we get into this case,
the more screamers seem to be tied up with Sarah's kidnapping. I guess we'd better call Lieutenant Babain and read her this message."

"Excuse me, guys—I don't mean to interrupt," Kareem said, swiveling in his chair to
face the Hardys, "but what are you—detectives? For a couple of dudes who just turned up
at a computer seminar, you sure are involved in
this case."

"Well, actually, we *are* detectives," Joe said
self-consciously. "Our dad, Fenton Hardy, is a
professional detective. And sometimes we help
him out. Like this time."

"Fenton Hardy." Kareem frowned. "I don't
recognize the name. Anyway," he said, "if you're
looking for suspects, there are others besides
Paulette who could threaten Evans with a
screamer virus if they wanted to."

"Like who?" Joe asked.

"Bruno Laird," one of the other technicians,
a short young man with curly red hair, spoke up.
"He's Evans's right-hand man. There's nothing
Evans does that he doesn't know about."

"And let's not forget Seethus," Kareem added.
"As chief of security, he'd have been told."

"I have an idea," said Frank. "Could you
guys run a computer check on the Evanco employees? It looks pretty certain that this is an
inside job. If anyone working here has an arrest
record or has any reason to resent J. P. Evans,
we should know."

"We can do that," said one of the technicians eagerly. "We're not supposed to, but we can."

"Great," said Frank. "And while you're at it, can you find out who else was involved with the screamers prevention project, too?"

"That's easy," the technician replied. "Everyone at Evanco is rated according to their security clearance. Clearance one means the employee knows everything Evans knows. Clearance two means they know all but the best-kept company secrets. Most of us are clearance three," he added. "Only clearance one employees would know all about screamers."

"Perfect!" Frank turned to his brother. "Let's find Dad. He might want to be with us when we call the police about the Comptellit message."

"Right." Frank turned toward the door. "Thanks, guys," he added with a wave. "We'll be back later for the results—and maybe we could also look at that videotape of the kidnapping."

"Glad to be of service," Kareem said.

"I'll walk you downstairs," the red-haired technician said suddenly. Before the Hardys could protest, he had jumped up from his chair and was walking them quickly to the stairs.

"My name's Buzz McKennon," he said in a low voice as he descended the stairs with the Hardys. Hastily he shook hands with both Frank and Joe. "I couldn't let you go without adding one more name to the list of people who know about the screamer virus. The biggest expert we have at Evanco was right in the control room."

"Who is it?" Joe asked, surprised.

"Kareem Addar," Buzz answered.

The Hardys stared at him.

"He's the guy in charge of destroying the virus," Buzz insisted. "What I thought you guys should know is, the only person who knows more about screamers than Kareem is the person who invented them."

As they rode the elevator down, the boys discussed what Buzz McKennon had just told them. "First we find out Paulette is lying," Frank said, "and we don't know how much or why. Then it turns out Kareem Addar is keeping secrets from us, too."

"I know," Joe said. "Does everyone connected to Evanco have something to hide?" He stopped talking as the elevator doors opened to let some people on.

"Dad's probably eating lunch by now," Frank said as the elevator descended to the main floor. "Let's see if we can catch him."

"Fine with me," Joe said as the elevator doors opened. "I could eat a couple of burgers by now, and then wash them down with a hero."

Joe led the way out of the elevator, and stopped at the information desk to find out what floor the company cafeteria was on. Then they went to a different bank of elevators and rode to the fifth floor.

Joe wasn't surprised to find that Evanco's employee cafeteria was as tastefully decorated as the rest of the building. Small, modern oak tables were scattered around the large, carpeted space. Soothing music played on the loudspeakers, and men and women sat eating a variety of dishes.

"There he is." Frank pointed to the cafeteria-style serving line at one end of the room. Joe spotted Fenton Hardy chatting with Mr. Lindquist, who stood behind him in line. When Fenton saw his sons, he waved them over.

"There you are, boys," he said as Frank and Joe approached him. "What have you been up to the last few hours?"

"Well, let's see," Joe said with a glance at the public relations director. "We've been arrested, contacted by the kidnappers, and lied to by just about everyone. Other than that, it's been pretty quiet. How about you?"

"You saw the Comptellit message, then?" their father said, not looking surprised.

"Yes," said Joe with a stab of disappointment. "How'd you know about it so soon?"

"The message was printed out on every computer at police headquarters, as well as at all the local papers," Lindquist told him. "No one knows who sent it, but it's going to be front-page news tomorrow."

Lindquist shook his head in concern. "I've had to deal with plenty of threats to Evanco's reputation in the past," he said to the Hardys, "but I've never had to explain to reporters why J. P. Evans might want to kidnap his daughter."

"Speaking of explanations," Fenton said, "what's this about being arrested?"

"It's a long story," Frank said. Joe knew his brother didn't want to bring up what had happened with Paulette while Lindquist was listening. "Anyway, the charges were dropped. The important thing for us is find Sarah's kidnapper. It's been nearly twenty hours since she disappeared, and anything could have happened to her."

"Do you think there's any chance that Evans *did* kidnap his daughter?" Joe asked Lindquist.

"Certainly not!" the Evanco executive replied. "Obviously, that message was left by the kidnappers themselves, to put the investigators off the track."

"If that's true, it means the kidnappers know about screamers," Frank pointed out. "That would probably mean that at least one of them was working at Evanco. Do you have any suggestions on who, sir?"

Lindquist reddened, then turned away without answering.

Fenton Hardy said in a low voice to his sons, "Maybe I should follow up on the Comptellit lead. Meanwhile, you boys might try to track down the source of the kidnappers' rubber masks. Lieutenant Babain tells me her department hasn't had any luck with that so far."

"Sure." Joe's eyes were on the menu board. "But first things first. Let's eat!"

Frank and Joe took a cab to the part of Chicago known as the Loop in search of masks like the kidnappers'. Despite the wind and cold, they enjoyed wandering past the many shops. Each time they spotted a shop that might sell masks, Joe and Frank ducked inside to show their rubber sample to the clerk. But each time the shop clerk failed to come up with a match for that particular substance and was unable to identify what it was.

"I give up," Joe said finally as dusk began to fall. "There must be over half a dozen shops that sell masks, and we've tried them all. The kidnappers must have bought their masks out of town."

"Wait." Frank pointed to a brightly painted sign down the street. "There's one we missed." As the boys approached the store, Frank read aloud from the sign, " 'American Costume and Theatrical Supply House.' We might as well give it a try."

Once inside, Joe saw that the costume shop was dark and cluttered. Its walls were draped with masks, costumes, and posters. A middle-aged, white-haired man stood behind the counter, entering numbers into a ledger.

"Yes, gentlemen," he said, looking up as the Hardys entered. "Andrew Nelson at your service. How may I help you this evening?"

Presenting the scrap of rubber to the store owner, Frank asked if the shop carried masks of similar material. "In a shop like mine?" Mr. Nelson tested the texture with his fingers. "Surely you're joking."

"We're not," Frank said in surprise. "We saw some masks like this in a—a theater performance, and we decided we wanted some like them for a play we're doing."

Nelson eyed the Hardys skeptically. "Your producers must be very rich if you're considering masks like this. This material comes from the latest computerized technology. I do makeup for TV productions sometimes, and I saw a mask made like this once. What they do is use a computer scanner to input the exact dimensions of a human face into a computer, and then the computer directs the mask-making machine to build a new, rubber face for that person."

He held the rubber out for the Hardys to inspect. "This latex is so thin that it's almost like a layer of real skin. They can make an actor look like whoever they want. You could be six inches away from a person in one of these masks and not know he was wearing one."

"Wow," Joe said. "Do you know anyone who makes them?"

Nelson fingered the scrap of rubber thoughtfully. "No, I don't," he said. "Most of the computers devoted to this kind of thing are in Hollywood. Oh, wait," he said, his expression changing suddenly. "I did see something about this recently, at the Museum of Technology and Science downtown. They've set up an exhibit on movie-making, and this type of mask-making program is included."

Joe sighed. What could a museum exhibit have to do with the kidnappers? he wondered. Nevertheless, he and Frank thanked Mr. Nelson and left the shop.

"That was interesting—if not very helpful," Joe said as they started down the sidewalk outside. Now that the sun had set, the temperature was plunging sharply. Joe shivered and put up the collar of his jacket. "Do you think we should check out the museum exhibit, or go on to something else?"

Frank looked at his watch. "I think the museum has closed already," he said. "We could try to track down Taylor Hayes, the Evanco executive Bruno Laird told us about," Frank suggested. "Come to think of it, he could easily be the one who left that message for Evans on Comptellit."

"You're right," said Joe, snapping his fingers. "And as a top executive at Evanco, he probably would have known about the screamers before he left the company."

"Laird said he was a computer wizard," Frank agreed. "Who knows—he might have figured out how to program the virus himself!"

The Hardys walked faster down the sidewalk, looking for a cab, but at that hour all the taxis were occupied by office workers headed home. As Frank and Joe rounded a corner onto a wider street, they were surprised to see a long black limousine slide up to the curb beside them.

"What's this?" Joe muttered. "Our driver?"

The Hardys watched as two large men in woolen overcoats got out. "It's Conrad Seethus," Joe said in a low voice. Then he called out to the bald man. "What's going on, Mr. Seethus? Did our dad tell you where we were?"

"Your dad has nothing to do with this," See-thus said gruffly. "I was sent to find you, and that's what I've done."

Frank was beginning to get a bad feeling as Seethus and his partner split up to come at the boys from opposite sides. Frank had seen this move before—a pincer attack. When he turned to Joe, he could see that his brother had had the same realization. The boys instantly turned, ready to run. They were shocked to see that a second black limousine had silently pulled up behind them. Several men got out of the car. Before either Joe or Frank could push their way past these men, they were grabbed from behind by Seethus and the men accompanying him. They hustled Frank and Joe around to the passenger side of the limousine. Pushing the Hardys into the front seat, Seethus added, "It's J. P. Evans. He wants to talk to you."

Chapter

9

JOE LANDED ON the front seat, stunned, as Frank tumbled in beside him. The passenger door slammed shut, and Joe realized that the car's keys were missing and that Seethus and his companion were standing guard outside.

Just then Joe heard a tinny voice come from somewhere in the car. "Hello, boys," the voice said. "Make yourselves at home. I won't keep you long. I just want a little information."

Joe looked around to see where the voice was coming from. "It's the speakerphone," Frank told him, pointing to a small box near the driver's seat.

Joe turned to look into the back of the car. The glass partition was tinted dark gray, as were the windows, but the divider was partially open, and Joe could make out a small, elderly man with white hair leaning back against the leather seat. Joe noted that the man was wearing white gloves. "I'm sorry we're forced to meet under these circumstances," Mr. Evans said. "My public relations man, Paul Lindquist, told me I might find you two here. He also tells me that you boys were suggesting to your father that I might have kidnapped my daughter."

"No, sir!" Joe said. "We just said—there was a message on the Comptellit network, and we—"

"I know all about that message," Evans snapped. "Listen to me, young man. That was the work of some crank—or worse, one of my many enemies. One doesn't get to be in my position without knowing plenty of people who'd love a chance at revenge. Of course I didn't kidnap my own daughter! In fact, I'd been looking forward to reuniting with her after two years before I was detained in Australia."

Joe looked at his brother. "Mr. Evans," Frank said, turning slightly to get a glimpse of the man in the semidarkness of the backseat, "if one of your enemies did leave the message, can you tell us who you think it might have been— and why they'd try to frame you for a kidnapping you didn't commit?"

"I certainly have my ideas," Evans snapped, crossing his gloved hands on his knee. "First among them is Sarah's roommate, Paulette Cameron."

"Paulette?" Joe repeated, surprised.

"Certainly," Evans said. "Paulette is what they call a computer radical. She believes software should be shared, free, with anyone who can't afford it, and she hates me because I've built my business on selling software at whatever price the market will bear. She's the one who turned Sarah against me, shortly after they met at college. Until recently I thought I'd lost my daughter forever. But then she changed her mind again and decided she trusted me more than Paulette.''

"What happened to make her change her mind?'' Frank asked.

Evans frowned. "That's not important. What *is* important is that that Cameron girl would stop at nothing to get Sarah back on her side. Without Sarah, you see, Paulette has nothing—no money, no influence. Paulette Cameron probably engineered Sarah's kidnapping herself, with a few of her radical friends. How else can she keep up her war against me, unless she maintains control of my daughter?''

"Hmm.'' Frank pulled back from the partition. He glanced at Joe, who shrugged in bewilderment. Back to Paulette again, Joe was thinking. Paulette blames Evans for the kidnapping, Laird thinks the culprit might be Taylor Hayes, and now Evans is blaming Paulette! How can we ever figure out which one is telling the truth?

"Mr. Laird tells me that you boys, along with your father, are excellent detectives,'' Evans said, interrupting Joe's thoughts. "I also understand you both are interested in summer jobs. We in the computer industry are used to respecting the minds of brilliant young people, and I am very, very anxious to be reunited with my daughter. Therefore, if you boys are able to catch Paulette Cameron in this kidnapping attempt and bring her to an arrest and conviction, I am prepared to offer you both the positions of your choice within my company." Thoughtfully, Evans tugged on his ear. "In fact," he added, "I can also promise to beat whatever salary you may be offered elsewhere."

Before the Hardys could respond, Evans tapped on the outside window with one gloved hand. The front passenger door of the limousine instantly opened, and Conrad Seethus leaned into the front seat.

"We're finished with our talk now," Mr. Evans said.

"Wait," Joe said, peering through the opening of the partition. "Mr. Evans, we'll do our best to catch the kidnappers. But we can't guarantee Paulette Cameron is the person we're looking for."

"She is," Evans said. "Now go."

The Hardys watched from the curb, astonished, as Seethus and his companion climbed into the front of the black limousine and it sped away into the night, followed by the second one. "Boy," Joe said, "that was strange. Do you believe what he said about Paulette, Frank?"

"It's possible," Frank said with a shrug. "Just as possible as what Paulette said about

Evans. But we're still not any closer to solving this case."

"You're right," Joe agreed. "We need to talk to some of the other suspects. I say we hunt down Taylor Hayes."

Frank put his hands in his jacket pockets and shook his head. "It's getting pretty late," he said. "Maybe we'd better put Hayes off until tomorrow. But we still have time to go back to EXacT network's control center, have a look at the employee files, and review the videotape of the kidnapping."

"Good idea." Joe spotted an empty cab and hailed it. "And after that, we eat again! There's something about hunting down a suspect that always increases my appetite."

This time when the Hardys climbed the stairs to the EXacT network control center, they found both Kareem and the redheaded technician, Buzz McKennon, gone. In their places were a pair of middle-aged men. When Frank asked whether Kareem Addar had left a message for them, both men insisted that the Hardys produce identification before they handed over a slim manila file folder.

"You'll have to read it up here," the engineer said to Frank. "Kareem says this is confidential information and is not to leave the control center."

Frank nodded, sat down in one of the swivel chairs, and opened the folder. Joe took a chair next to Frank and peered over his shoulder.

The folder held a single sheet of computer paper with a list of names printed on it. Joe's eyes ran quickly down the list. There wasn't a name there, he realized, that he didn't already know.

"J. P. Evans, Bruno Laird, Paul Lindquist, Taylor Hayes, Conrad Seethus . . . These are the only people at Evanco who know about the screamers?" Frank asked incredulously.

"At least they're the only people Kareem wants us to know about," Joe pointed out. "Look—he didn't include his own name, even though Buzz said he's in charge of the whole antivirus program."

"That *is* strange," Frank agreed. He frowned as he closed the folder. "Thanks a lot," he said to the engineer, returning the file. "Kareem had also told us we could look at the videotape of Sarah Evans's kidnapping. Would you mind showing it to us now?"

The two technicians exchanged an annoyed glance, but finally the first one pulled himself out of his chair and approached the video equipment in its U-shaped island in the center of the room. "Whatever you say, mister," the engineer said sarcastically. "Of course, we've got nothing better to do than wait on kids from out of town."

Joe was too interested in studying the videotape to pay attention to the disgruntled man. As the images of Sarah and her kidnappers appeared on the screen, he and Frank leaned forward to get a better look.

"There's no way we can identify them," Joe said. "They have those high-tech masks on, and the guy at the mask store says there's no way to tell what a person looks like underneath."

"Keep looking," Frank muttered, peering at the screen. "You never know what might turn up if you stare long enough."

Joe kept looking. As the kidnappers pushed past Kareem, tied up on his swivel chair but still kicking, they moved right in front of the surveillance camera. Since the camera hung from the ceiling of the room, it looked down at the kidnappers' heads.

"Hey, wait a minute," Joe said, putting a hand on the technician's arm so that he stopped the tape. "Look at that guy's head. Not the one with the eyepatch, but the other one."

"What?" said Frank, looking closer. "I don't see anything."

"Look at his hairline," Joe insisted. "Doesn't it look crooked? Like maybe it's a wig?"

"Wait a minute," said the technician, becoming interested in spite of himself. "I can zoom in on this. It's digitally recorded, you know—only the best for Evanco."

The Hardys watched excitedly as the man zoomed in on the image of the kidnapper's head. Joe's face lit up as he saw that the man's hairline was indeed crooked. In fact, both Hardys could now see that, in the space where the wig had been knocked back, an entire section of naked forehead had been revealed.

"Either that man has a very seriously receding

hairline,'' Frank said slowly, ''or under the wig he's completely bald.''

He and Joe turned to look at each other. ''And except for Kareem, who shaves his head, we've met only one other bald person,'' Joe finished for his brother. ''Conrad Seethus!''

Chapter

10

"CONRAD SEETHUS, the head of security, betraying his own boss," Joe said as the Hardys rode down in the elevator again.

"Not necessarily," Frank corrected him. "Seethus might have been operating under his boss's instructions. But the bald man on the video is built the same as Seethus. It looks like we have one of our men."

"Where did he say he was when the kidnapping happened?" Joe tried to recall. "Oh, I know—he said he was on his way home. Perfect. No one would be able to check on his alibi."

"Okay, so what do we have so far?" Frank said, running through the theories. "First, Conrad Seethus and one other man kidnapped Sarah Evans from the reception room—on their own or on someone's orders, we're not sure which."

"They took her up to the roof, where the helicopter they'd hijacked was waiting," Joe continued. "They bundled Sarah into the helicopter, and then one of them—I guess it was Seethus—nearly shot me."

"They flew to Indiana," Frank said, "dumped the helicopter with the pilot in it, and disappeared with Sarah."

Frank shook his head dejectedly. "Even if we're pretty sure one of the kidnappers was Conrad Seethus, we're no closer to knowing why he snatched her or where she is now. What really bothers me is that as far as we know, there's still been no ransom note. It's starting to look pretty certain that whoever Conrad is working for really is interested in something more than money."

"But that includes nearly all our suspects," Joe said. "Paulette, Hayes, and Kareem could all be seeking revenge against Evans. Evans could be after his own daughter. Even Seethus might hold a grudge against Evans that we don't know about."

"That's true," Frank said thoughtfully. "I guess we're back where we started." He glanced up at the floor indicator. They were rapidly descending to the main floor. "We don't have enough evidence to go to the police yet. Maybe we should try to find this Taylor Hayes after all."

"I'm with you," Joe said eagerly. "Forget about eating. Let's go!"

* * *

Even though Frank had given Taylor Hayes's address to the taxi driver, he was surprised when the car pulled up to the edge of Lake Michigan. "This is Navy Pier?" he asked. "I guess I thought that was the name of a subdivision out in the suburbs."

"This is it," the taxi driver said. "Your friend must live in one of the houseboats here. Nasty places." He made a face. "Full of rats."

Frank looked out the window at the bobbing cabin cruisers tied up to the docks of a good-size, well-maintained marina. Actually, he thought, this looked like an exciting place to live—near the park, just off Lake Shore Drive, and with a spectacular view of the Chicago skyline. Still, he realized as he paid the driver and stepped out into the icy night wind, it might be more comfortable in the summer.

"Are you sure this is the place?" Joe asked as the Hardys walked against the wind down the boardwalk. "These boats look battened down for the winter. Only a crazy person would live on a boat in weather like this."

"That's what we're looking for, isn't it?" Frank argued. "A person crazy enough to kidnap Sarah Evans?" Just then he spotted a light shining from the porthole of one of the cruisers. It was a blue-and-white fifty-four-footer, with a flying bridge on top. Frank guessed it could sleep four to six people easily. The name on the stern was *Not So Much*.

"This is it," Frank said, reading the nameplate on the post where the boat was tied up.

"The boat's name was added to the address in Laird's Rolodex, but at the time I didn't know what it meant. What do we do now—knock?"

Joe shrugged, put a hand to his mouth, and called out Taylor Hayes's name. Then the brothers waited until, a moment later, Frank heard a shuffle on deck.

"Wow," Frank murmured as Hayes appeared in the bright light of the marina. "He really does look crazy. He must be a genius or a madman—or both."

Frank watched as Hayes, who had a thick gray beard and a shaggy mane of gray hair, pulled off his old-fashioned frameless reading glasses to peer at the brothers from the deck.

"Who are you?" he demanded. "What are you doing here?"

"Mr. Hayes?" Frank asked.

"Go away," the man growled, waving at the boys with both hands. "Get someone else to help with your homework."

Frank exchanged a look with Joe. "What do you mean?" he asked Hayes.

"All you business students are alike!" Hayes grumbled, turning to walk away. "If you want to know what it was like to run J. P. Evans's business for twenty years, why don't you go to work there? That should teach you a thing or two."

"Excuse me, sir!" Joe called after the man's retreating back. "We're not students."

Hayes halted, then turned slowly to face the

Hardys again. "No?" he said. "Then who are you?"

"I'm Frank Hardy, and this is my brother, Joe," Frank said. "We want to talk to you about Sarah Evans's kidnapping."

Frank could see that he now had Hayes's attention. "Better come in out of the cold," Hayes said gruffly. Then he turned and started inside.

Quickly the Hardys boarded the cabin cruiser and followed Hayes down several steps into the main cabin.

Frank was surprised at how cozy and welcoming the boat was on the inside. With its overstuffed furniture, brass lamps, and glass-fronted bookcases, it was impossible to tell this was the cabin of a boat and not the living room of a regular house.

"Welcome," Hayes said as the Hardys unzipped their jackets. "Have a seat. Make yourselves at home. I apologize for having been rude before. You wouldn't believe how many people still harass me in my retirement—as though I knew a magic formula for getting rich in business! To tell you the truth, I don't have many fond memories of Evanco. I'm sixty-three years old, and that company betrayed me."

Frank nodded. "I understand you had a falling out with Mr. Evans," he said.

"A falling out!" Hayes repeated bitterly. "That's certainly an understatement. The man literally threw me out into the street."

"Why was that, Mr. Hayes?" Joe asked, leaning forward eagerly.

Hayes closed his eyes against the memory. "Most of our disagreement had to do with something that remains confidential," he said quietly. "Suffice it to say that Evanco had received an offer to buy a program that would ultimately prove useful for nothing but destructive purposes. I wanted to turn down the proposal or perhaps pay the program's creator to destroy the program. Evans, on the other hand, was determined to own the program. I believe he planned to use it to threaten his competitors."

Frank's pulse raced as he, too, leaned forward in his chair. "Mr. Hayes," he asked, "could this program possibly be for a computer virus called screamers?"

Hayes's eyes opened wide in surprise. "Yes," he admitted, looking from one Hardy to the other. "How did you know?"

"We suspect that the screamers are linked somehow to Sarah's kidnapping," Frank told him. "We need to know who among the people familiar with the program might have a motive for kidnapping Sarah."

Hayes laughed weakly. "There were so many, if you count those with a grudge against J.P."

"How about Paulette Cameron?" Joe asked.

Hayes nodded thoughtfully. "Paulette is a strange girl," he admitted. "It's true she loathed Evans, and all he stood for. I understand she turned Sarah against her father when she and Sarah first became friends. The two of them were bent on destroying Evanco by whatever means necessary."

Hayes leaned back in his chair. "But then something extraordinary happened," he told the boys. "Paulette was making giant strides in her programming abilities at school. And she invented a new kind of program—a virus that can make a computer explode."

Frank stared at the gray-haired man, his mind reeling. "Paulette Cameron *invented* the screamers virus?"

Hayes smiled wanly. "It was a terrible time for her," he told Frank. "On the one hand, she hated Evans, and Evanco, too. On the other hand, she stood to make millions if she sold her program to Evans. He even offered her a top position in the company. It was all she could do to refuse."

"Did Sarah know about this?" Joe asked.

"Not at first," Hayes told him. "Eventually, after Paulette had turned Evans down, she told Sarah about the virus. But by then it was too late. Evanco's own top programmer, a brilliant young man named Kareem Addar, had figured out the key to the screamers virus himself. Evans no longer needed Paulette—or her program. That, by the way, is when I was fired," he added. "I opposed the use of the virus. I believe it is extremely dangerous and its use is highly immoral. Evans, obviously, disagreed."

"Wow." Frank sank back against the cushions of the chair. "At last it's beginning to make sense! So then," he ventured, "Sarah and Paulette must have tried to figure out a way to convince Evans not to use the screamers program."

"That's what I assume," Hayes replied. "Of course, the rest of the story I know only from educated guesses and assorted gossip. But it did make sense to me when I heard that Sarah and J.P. had arranged some kind of reunion. J.P.'s getting old, and I know he misses his daughter. And our Sarah is quite a smart girl herself. I feel sure she agreed to stop the feud with her father if he would agree to destroy the screamers program once and for all."

"And Paulette went along to the reception to make sure he kept the promise," Joe suggested. "That explains why Paulette acted so weirdly with us. She wanted us to go after Evans, who she thought kidnapped Sarah. But she didn't want the police involved because they might find out about her role in the screamers project. So she threatened Evans over the Comptellit network, and she led us to discover the message in the hopes that we would lead the cops to Evans."

"But it still doesn't explain why Evans didn't show up at the reception to reunite with his daughter," Frank pointed out. "And we still don't really know which of the people involved is behind Sarah's kidnapping—or why."

Hayes listened closely, then took a deep breath, as though thinking before saying, "I, too, am terribly worried about Sarah. I knew her well for many years. I wasn't able to sleep last night, worrying about what might have happened to her. If I knew any more that might help get her back, I'd tell you and anyone else who asked.''

"There *is* one thing you might help us with," Frank said cautiously. "We think Conrad Seethus might have been involved in the kidnapping. Do you think he would have organized to do it on his own?"

"Seethus? Are you kidding?" Hayes snorted in derision, and Frank saw a look of relief cross his face at this change in subject. "Seethus is nothing but a yes-man, programmed to say yes to whoever happens to be ordering him about. When he worked for me, he said yes to every order I gave him. Now I'm sure he's saying yes to—''

Hayes's sentence was interrupted by the ear-splitting noise of shattering glass.

"Duck!" Frank yelled as the porthole behind Hayes exploded.

As Hayes and the Hardys dove for the floor, bullets ripped into the boat, filling the cabin with glass, splinters, and dust.

Chapter

11

"FRANK! He's shot!" Joe crawled over to where Hayes lay bleeding and barely conscious. The firing stopped as suddenly as it had started. In the eerie silence that followed, Joe ripped back Hayes's shirt to make sure he was still breathing. A bullet had apparently lodged in the man's side. Joe looked around wildly for something to use as a bandage. Frank appeared just then with a towel that had been left on one of the chairs. Joe grabbed it and wrapped it around Hayes's waist.

"You stay with him," Joe whispered to Frank. "I'm going on deck to see what's up."

Before Frank could stop him, Joe started up the stairs.

But as soon as Joe arrived on deck, he realized he was too late. A small man with an AK-47 was racing down the boardwalk toward the parking lot of the marina. Even as Joe reached the dock, the man dived into a battered-looking blue compact car. The shooting had brought several other people onto the decks of their cabin cruisers and the veranda of the marina's office building.

"Call an ambulance," Joe shouted to the onlookers. "A man's been wounded here!" Then he raced down the dock toward the gunman's car. Long before he reached the parking lot, the car backed up and sped away, its tires squealing. Joe stopped, trying to make out the license plate number in the darkness of the pier, when suddenly the car skidded on a slick spot on the pavement. Joe watched, stunned, as the vehicle spun out of control and smashed into a lamppost.

Now I've got you, Joe thought as he began to run again. The car's left front fender was crumpled, and a tire was blown. There was no way the gunman would get away now.

"Somebody call the police!" Joe yelled as he neared the car. As he ran, Joe saw the car door fly open and the gunman pull himself out from behind the wheel. The man pointed his weapon directly at Joe.

Joe froze and stared at the weapon.

Slowly, as if in a dream, the gunman smiled and pulled the trigger. Joe stared into the muzzle of the weapon, waiting to see the flash of light.

But nothing happened.

Gradually Joe realized that the weapon was

jammed. Reacting instinctively, he found himself running to tackle the gunman before he could unjam the weapon. Instead the gunman dropped the AK-47 and sprinted away.

Joe raced after the man, ready to duck at any moment in case his assailant was concealing a second gun. Running at an astonishing speed, the gunman raced across Lake Shore Drive and into a stand of trees. Joe pushed himself to run faster, wondering at the same time whether or not Hayes had survived. He *had* to catch the gunman, Joe thought, not only because of Hayes, but also because the man might be one of the kidnapping suspects.

Where can he be going? Joe wondered a moment later as he followed the man onto an open field. A huge, dark shape loomed out of the darkness at the field's opposite end, and the gunman seemed to be headed straight toward it.

When Joe saw what the shape was, he nearly tripped over his own shoes. The gunman was nearing an enormous submarine beached on dry land. When the man reached the submarine, though, he ran around it.

"What is going on?" Joe gasped the words as he, too, reached the submarine. Propped up with steel supports, it looked spooky in the moonlight. Ahead, Joe could see the gunman running past what looked like a diesel train locomotive and several passenger-train cars.

Out of breath, Joe forced himself to follow the gunman. As he passed the train, he realized it was sitting in a large parking lot. Now the gunman headed toward a large building adjacent to the lot. A single light shone over the building's back door. Silently, Joe read the sign nailed up beneath the light: Loading Dock. Museum of Technology and Science. Authorized Personnel Only.

Museum of Technology and Science, Joe mused as he ran. Where had he heard that name today? Now, he saw the gunman ducking around the old-fashioned train and heading straight for the building.

"Oh, no," Joe breathed, throwing his energy into a last desperate sprint. "You're not getting away now!"

"Hang in there, buddy," Frank heard a paramedic say to Taylor Hayes as she and her partner lifted the wounded man onto a stretcher. Frank studied Hayes, but the man's eyes remained closed. Six police officers in three cars had already arrived by the time the ambulance had driven up to the pier. The marina was a festival of flashing lights and staring neighbors that left Frank feeling dazed.

"Can you give us a description of the gunman?" a uniformed officer was asking Frank, who stood near the stretcher.

"I told you," Frank said, trying to focus on what he was saying, "I didn't see the gunman, but my brother ran off after him. You need to find them before it's too late!"

Frank turned to talk to the other officers standing nearby when suddenly he felt a tug on his sleeve. He looked down to see that Hayes had gripped it.

"Mr. Hayes?" Frank said, squatting down to the man's level on the stretcher. "You wanted to say something to me?"

Frank watched as Hayes struggled to speak. "P-Paulette," he stammered. "T-tell Paulette I need to talk to her."

Frank nodded.

"She—she has to quit what she's doing," Hayes said with a gasp. "T-too dangerous."

"And Evans?" Frank asked quickly, glancing at the worried-looking paramedics. "Any message for him?"

Hayes strained, his face white as the sheet that covered him. "Evans—" he said, "may be in trouble, too. Could—could have been . . . murdered."

Stunned, Frank moved closer to Hayes, hoping to hear an explanation. But the wounded man began to choke, and the paramedics instantly moved in to carry him to the ambulance. Bewildered, Frank followed the stretcher to the ambulance and watched Hayes carefully as he was loaded in.

At the last minute, as the paramedics were about to close the ambulance doors, Frank saw the older man gesture feebly toward him. Despite the protests of the paramedics, Frank leapt into the back of the ambulance and again put his ear close to Hayes's mouth.

"Be careful," the man rasped, his words

barely audible. "They know you and Joe have talked to me."

"*Who* knows?" Frank demanded. "Tell me!"

Hayes's eyelids fluttered. A paramedic tried unsuccessfully to pull Frank away. Then Hayes began to speak again.

"L-Laird," came the rasping voice. "He's spying—"

Hayes's voice drifted off. "Come on, kid, that's enough," the paramedic said, pulling at Frank more forcefully this time. "He's too weak to talk any more, can't you see that?"

Frank nodded and climbed out of the ambulance. The paramedics shut the doors, and a moment later the ambulance took off.

"We sent a team after your brother and the gunman," the police officer told Frank as an unmarked car with a patrol light on top took the ambulance's place on the dock. "Don't worry, kid. We'll find them."

"I hope so." Frank watched the passengers of the new car step out onto the dock. He recognized Lieutenant Babain and Officer Adler.

"Hello, kid," Lieutenant Babain said, striding over to have a look at Frank. "No wounds at all, I see. You're very lucky. From what I hear, your friend Hayes might not make it."

"I don't want to talk about it!" Frank snapped uncharacteristically. "All I want you to do is find my brother."

"These police here will take care of that," Babain told him. "Meanwhile let's have a look at the wrecked car in the parking lot. While we're walking there, you can tell me exactly why you and your brother were hanging out around the pier.''

As they walked toward the boardwalk, Frank told Babain what he and Joe had been up to that day. He explained about Kareem Addar and Paulette Cameron, about the mask material, and the list of Evanco employees. By the time they reached the car, even Babain was wide-eyed at the possibilities.

''You guys haven't wasted time,'' she admitted. ''I'd say you've come up with more information than the FBI. The only lead they had to offer so far was that there were traces of oil and anthracite dust on the floor of the kidnappers' chopper.''

''Anthracite?'' Frank asked. ''You mean coal?''

''You got it. Doesn't compute, right?'' Babain sighed. ''Anyway, I wish I had your leads to take back to my boss.''

''Take them,'' Frank said generously. ''Joe and I don't care about the credit. We just want to rescue Sarah.''

''We'll see,'' she said, her attitude growing formal once again. ''Let's check out the vehicle.''

Frank saw that there were already two police officers examining the blue car, but they didn't try to stop the lieutenant and Frank from taking a look as well.

Frank saw to his disappointment that the car was perfectly neat and clean. There was no trash, no personal papers, nothing to give away the identity of the mysterious gunman.

"Joe and I believe there's more to this kidnapping than just holding Sarah for ransom," Frank said, sticking his head behind the steering wheel.

"Like what?" Babain asked from the backseat. "This exploding computer thing?"

"Like this, maybe," Frank replied. He pulled something out from under the crunched steering column. He held it out to Babain.

"What is it?" the lieutenant asked as she took the object from Frank. Together they looked down at the torn fragment of rubber in her hand. It was nearly as thin as a layer of skin, Frank noted, and was covered with very realistic-looking wrinkles.

"Wherever there's trouble, there are these masks," he said. "Find the computer that's making the masks, and I bet you can find the kidnappers."

"Yeah," Babain said uncertainly, looking from the bit of rubber to Frank. "You think your brother's all right?"

Frank shrugged. He had been worrying about the same thing and trying not to. Where was Joe?

Joe slipped inside the back door of the Museum of Technology and Science as silently as he possibly could. The gunman had entered a moment earlier, unlocking the door with a key, and before the door closed completely Joe had managed to slip one foot inside. Now he moved quietly into a darkened room, expecting to be attacked at any moment.

This is just like a horror movie, Joe thought as he tried to make out the dark shapes of the exhibits in the large, open museum gallery. Barely illuminated by the red Exit signs at the doors, rockets, model nuclear power stations, and X-ray machines loomed menacingly.

Suddenly Joe heard a noise about halfway across the gallery. He hurried past the exhibits toward the source of the noise. He paused beside a model of one of the first supercomputers, and his attention was drawn to the thirty-year-old machine right out of an old science-fiction movie.

"The K.A.L. 5000," read a black-and-white sign beside the computer, "originally built by Dr. Arthur Charles Ludwig, is the basis on which all modern computers evolved. This model was graciously reconstructed for the museum by Dr. Ludwig himself."

Joe heard another sound—this time several hundred feet away. He slid away from the supercomputer, keeping low to the ground as he trailed the gunman across the gallery. He hoped Frank had managed to send the police after them. Would they think to look inside the museum? Joe wondered. And if they did, would it be too late?

Suddenly an enormous, gaping hole opened up before Joe. He stopped in his tracks, barely stifling a gasp. By the dim light, he read a sign telling him that the hole was a working replica of a coal mine. Visitors started their tour with an open-car elevator ride down into the "mine," which was built with actual rock and coal and filled with authentic drilling equipment.

Joe contemplated the mine entrance for a moment, unsure what to do. The sudden noise of a machine switching on caused him to jump with fright. He realized in the next instant that the coal mine's elevator was in operation. The gunman was going down!

Instinctively Joe leapt through the dark toward the elevator, landing with a thud on the roof of the open-side box. Hoping that the noise of the elevator had drowned out the noise of his landing, Joe squatted on the roof as the elevator went down the coal shaft. It really felt as if they were sinking into the earth, he thought. He could smell the cool, damp rock on all sides.

A moment later, the elevator car reached bottom, and Joe heard footsteps moving away from it. He waited a long moment, holding his breath. Then, as silently as possible, he lifted the trapdoor in the elevator's roof and slid down inside the car. From there it was easy to slip into the interior of the coal mine.

Joe stood still a few steps from the elevator and squinted into the darkness. The park outside had seemed dark, he realized, and the gallery upstairs even darker. But this fake coal mine was the darkest place he had ever seen. He held his hand in front of his face. He couldn't see anything.

Nervously, Joe moved so that his back was against a stone wall of the shaft. His head was racing. Was the gunman still running, he wondered—or had he led Joe down here to ambush him?

Either way, it didn't matter, Joe realized. He was still trapped in this pit with a potential killer.

Chapter

12

JOE KEPT HIS BACK against the wall, ordering himself not to panic. As silently as possible, he began moving.

After what seemed like an eternity, Joe felt the rock wall behind him end in a metal slab. Joe felt a heavy steel door set into the metal. His hands groped for the doorknob. He expected it to be locked, but the knob turned under his fingers.

Okay, Joe said silently to the gunman. Where are you? Waiting for me to go through the door so you can blast me?

The heat in the mine shaft was oppressive, and Joe felt sweat beading on his forehead as he slowly pulled the door open. He slipped through the door and closed it quickly behind him, then threw himself across the chamber.

For a long moment, Joe waited for the sound of bullets, but only silence greeted him. Finally he dared to look around. Faint lights in the distance provided a small degree of illumination.

He was out of the mine exhibit—that much was clear. Joe guessed he must have stepped through some sort of maintenance exit. Ahead lay a narrow, dimly lit corridor. Since he hadn't heard the door open or close before him, Joe assumed the killer hadn't come this way. Nevertheless, he was cautious as he made his way down the hall.

As he walked, his shoes stuck to the floor a little, as if there was gummy oil on the floor's surface. It was too dark to tell what the substance was. He glanced warily at the doors he passed in the corridor. The doors probably led to supply closets, Joe thought, but the gunman just might be hiding behind one.

Finally Joe arrived at an intersection. In the faint light, he looked to his left down the new hall, then to his right. The new corridor seemed empty, too. Joe realized there must be a maze of maintenance corridors beneath the main gallery. He wondered if there was a back way to the upper level. He kept walking straight, when—

Whump! Joe heard a noise behind him and started to turn, but he was too late. A blow caught him across the back of the head, sending him crumpling to the floor. He could hear footsteps running away and the vague sound of a voice in the distance. But he couldn't quite hear what the voice was saying.

"Oh," Joe moaned, struggling to pull himself back to his feet. His head was pounding. He felt the back of his head and was relieved to discover it wasn't bleeding.

"Hey, kid!"

Joe jumped as a hand grabbed his shoulder. He spun around and nearly brained the man behind him with a punch. Just in time, though, he saw that the man was far too old to be his gunman. Joe pulled back his arm and leaned against the wall in relief and exhaustion.

"Hold on, there," said the old man. In the dim light, Joe could see that the man was white-haired and wore a baggy cardigan sweater.

"Sorry," Joe said, still shaken. "But would you mind telling me—who are you?"

The man grunted. "I was about to ask you the same question. What are you doing down here?"

"I—I'm after somebody. And I think he just clobbered me," Joe said.

"After somebody, eh? What do you mean?"

"A man with a gun," Joe explained. "He just shot someone."

"And you followed him *here?*" the man asked.

"Yes," Joe said. "Did you pass anyone?"

"No. Sorry." The man shook his head. "I'm Charlie Ludwig. I work around here."

Joe recognized the name. "Dr. Ludwig? The computer guy? I'm Joe Hardy."

"Yes," the man said. "You saw my computer exhibit, I suppose. It's not quite finished yet, actually. I'll be up all night getting it working. I haven't worked on a 5000 in nearly fifteen years!"

Joe nodded, wondering how many computer experts he'd have to meet before he solved this case.

"Let's get out of here," the scientist suggested. "We'll go back to my office and call someone to come check you out. And you can tell me all about your little adventure."

"Actually, I need to use the telephone," Joe said, thinking of how worried Frank must be by now.

"No problem. You can use the one in my office," said Ludwig, leading him to the end of the corridor and through another door. The new hall they entered was better lit, and Ludwig turned to inspect Joe.

"You don't look so good, if you don't mind my saying so," Ludwig said. "I have some cold juice. That should get your blood sugar racing."

Ludwig turned and headed for the first door in the corridor. He opened it, revealing a small office with a wooden desk, a personal computer, and stacks of books and papers. He stood back, waiting for Joe to enter, and tugged on his earlobe nervously.

That's funny, Joe thought, eyeing the scientist. So many people in this town have the same nervous habit. Did J. P. Evans influence Ludwig to start tugging at his earlobe? Or is it just something scientists do?

Joe started for the door, then paused to look again at the scientist. Ludwig's eyes met Joe's passively, as if they were hiding something. As

Joe gazed at the oddly flat blue eyes, he felt as if he'd been hit by a lightning bolt.

"Um, on second thought," he said, backing away from the door, "my brother's out there, see, and there's still a gunman on the loose. I think I'd better get going and help him."

Before Ludwig could protest, Joe had run to the end of the corridor and up a flight of stairs to the gallery floor. He raced across the dark gallery, heedless now of any gunman, and out the back door. But the image of Ludwig tugging on his earlobe still made him shudder.

"There you are!" Frank cried when Joe appeared at the marina fifteen minutes later, flanked on either side by the pair of police officers he'd found searching for him around the beached submarine. "What happened? Lieutenant Babain and Officer Adler and I had just about given up on you. We were sitting around waiting to hear the shots."

"Very funny," Joe said. "The gunman got away. Did someone take Hayes to a hospital?"

"The ambulance left half an hour ago," the lieutenant told him. "Now I'd better get you back to the hotel and your dad. It's almost midnight."

By the time the Hardys reached their father's hotel room that night, they had managed a quick exchange of information and theories about the kidnapping. Joe was glad they'd had the chance to talk, brief as it was.

"Where have you been?" their father demanded as he opened the door to his sons. "I've had half the seminar out looking for you!"

"We've been following leads, Dad," Frank said quietly. Both he and Joe sat down on the bed.

"What leads are those?" Fenton demanded. "This had better be good."

"For one thing, we had a talk with J. P. Evans," Frank said casually. "He picked up Joe and me, and he told us he thinks Paulette Cameron has Sarah."

"J. P. Evans?" Mr. Hardy looked impressed. "No one meets him—no one except Bruno Laird."

Frank nodded. "That's point one of our hypothesis."

With a sigh, Fenton Hardy sat down in an armchair. "Okay, out with it," he said. "Give me your theory—because I know that unless you tell it to me, none of us will get any sleep."

"Number one, we believe J. P. Evans may have been murdered," Joe said.

"Murdered? Dead?" Fenton Hardy jumped halfway up from his chair, then sank back down. "How can he be dead? You said you just saw him this afternoon!"

"Good point," Frank said. "But Taylor Hayes thinks J.P. might have been killed, and Hayes may be right. After all, Evans supposedly returned to Chicago, but no one has seen him. We think someone was impersonating Evans this afternoon."

"Remember those masks, Dad?" Joe put in.

"We learned today that that particular kind of mask can make anyone look almost exactly like anyone else. They're almost like skin, and they can be worn all day. The impostor must have been wearing one when he was pretending to be J.P."

"All right," Fenton said cautiously to his sons. "Assuming you're right—go ahead."

"Point number two," Frank went on. "The FBI said the floor of the getaway chopper was mysteriously sprinkled with anthracite dust and gummy oil."

"And look," Joe added, showing his father the bottoms of his shoes. "This is a mix of coal dust and some very gummy stuff that I picked up in the coal mine exhibit at the Museum of Technology and Science today."

"So?" their father said, obviously not impressed with this news. "What does the Museum of Technology and Science have to do with a hijacked chopper?"

The phone on the bedside table rang. Mr. Hardy held up a finger to signal the boys to wait while he answered. Joe was impatient, wanting to tell his father that Ludwig the scientist had struck him as remarkably similar to both J. P. Evans and Bruno Laird. But his father's expression was turning from interested to grave. When Fenton Hardy hung up the phone, he looked stunned.

"That was one of the Evanco people," he said to his sons. "The computers in the Intensive Care Unit at Cook County Hospital just blew up, all at once. The explosions knocked out the power at the hospital and started some fires. People have been hurt.''

Frank rose to his feet. "What about Hayes?" he demanded. "That's the hospital he was sent to."

"I know." Mr. Hardy frowned. "Hayes is all right, but he was lucky. He was still unconscious, so he didn't even notice that the patients on either side of him died. Lieutenant Babain is putting him under protective custody now.''

"A little late for that," Joe muttered angrily.

"Don't blame the police," Mr. Hardy said to Joe. "Blame the kidnappers. They don't know when to stop."

That night Joe slept badly in his and Frank's hotel room, tossing and turning through nightmares featuring hidden gunmen and pitch-dark rooms. When Frank woke him up the next morning, Joe felt as though he hadn't slept at all.

"Can't I sleep in today?" he complained, stretching and then falling back against the pillows. "I've just about solved the case. You and Dad finish up, and we'll all meet for lunch.''

"You wish," Frank said, tiredly rubbing his eyes. Joe guessed that his brother hadn't slept well, either, and he instantly felt sorry for what he'd said.

"Come on, Joe. Dad's already waiting for us downstairs. We'll have breakfast, and then we'll go see Hayes at the hospital. After that, I'm hoping we can get in to talk to Laird.''

"Sounds good," Joe admitted. He headed toward the bathroom. "But if I'm not out in ten minutes," he added as he shut the door, "come in after me. I have a feeling I could fall asleep in the shower."

By eight o'clock Frank and Joe were showered and dressed and looking forward to the day's investigations. They grabbed their keys, wallets, and jackets and were heading for the door when they heard a knock on the other side.

"Uh-oh," Joe said, one hand frozen on the doorknob. "Do you think this is who I think it is?"

"Let her in," Frank said. "We promised to take her to see the chopper pilot today, remember? How can she know how much has changed?"

Joe opened the door, and Paulette burst into the room, already talking. "I just heard that Taylor Hayes is in the hospital!" she cried. "I can't believe it—that man never hurt anyone."

"We know all about it," Joe said. "In fact, Frank and I came close to joining him in intensive care."

"Speaking of which," Frank said, putting his hands on Paulette's shoulders and forcing her into one of the hotel room's chairs, "Joe and I have some questions to ask about the exploding computers at the hospital last night. Apparently, you know more about screamers than you've let on. And, from what we understand, you invented the virus in the first place!"

"I don't know what you're talking about," Paulette said curtly.

"Fine, then." Joe sat in the chair facing Paulette's. "We'll talk about Hayes. According to my brother, Hayes's last words before he was taken to the hospital were, 'Tell Paulette to stop.' Do you think he could possibly mean these computer explosions that keep happening? And what about your ransacked room? You did that yourself, didn't you—so we'd find the message on Comptellit and begin to suspect J. P. Evans of the crime."

Paulette looked down at her hands, which she was twisting in her lap. "Okay," she admitted at last. "I did try to fool you into thinking the kidnappers had torn up my room. And I did send out a few small screamers, just to shake things up—but not at the hospital. I'd never do that!"

Paulette turned a pleading gaze on Joe. "I had to show Evans and Laird that I meant business, don't you see? And I do. If they don't free Sarah by noon tomorrow, my screamers will destroy their entire business."

"Just their business?" Frank prodded. "Will the military bases go down, too? The airlines and hospitals and TV stations? Will the world stop because you want it to?"

"Of course not!" Paulette snapped. She spoke more quickly. "They're holding Sarah, don't you see? She was getting in the way of *their* using screamers against their enemies. Now she's no danger to them—she's locked up where no one can hear her. If I don't rescue her, who will?''

Frank turned to look at his brother. "I don't trust her," he said flatly. "Let's take her to the Evanco Building. We'll bring her with us to talk to Kareem Addar. Maybe between the two of them, we can get the story right.''

"I don't want to go," Paulette protested, struggling against Joe as he grasped her by the arm. "I hate Kareem Addar! He works for the enemy. Just when I thought I had Evans beaten down, he stole my program and reinvented it. I'll never speak to him again.''

"Come on," Joe said as gently as he could. "It won't take long. We want the same thing you do, Paulette. We want to see Sarah set free.''

Scowling, Paulette finally agreed to accompany them.

As usual, Joe heard rock music playing in the control center even before they reached the top of the stairs. He entered the room, followed by Frank and Paulette, to find Kareem at his post along with three other technicians.

"Hey, Joe!" Kareem said, spinning around in his chair as he saw Joe enter. But Joe saw his face freeze when Paulette entered the room.

"Oh," Kareem said dully. "It's you.''

"I told you I didn't want to come here," Paulette said loudly to Frank. "Now I want to go.''

"Wait a minute," Frank said sternly. "You and Kareem are supposed to have a conversation about the screamers and try to come up with a suspect for the screamers you didn't set."

"*You* caused some of those explosions?" Kareem said, staring at the girl. "But, Paulette," he chided sarcastically, "I thought you didn't believe in violence—unless it comes at the right price."

"Shut up, Kareem," Paulette spat out. "If anyone knows about creating violent toys for corporate computerland, it's you. You and I don't have anything to say to each other." Tearing her arm away from Frank's grip, Paulette turned to go.

"Paulette, wait!" Joe cried. "You aren't supposed to—"

Joe was interrupted by an enormous blast. "Hit the floor!" Joe yelled, pushing his brother back into the stairwell. Flying glass filled the air as every computer module in the control center blew.

Chapter

13

"KAREEM!" Joe shouted after the noise of shattering glass had ended. The stairs to the control center were enveloped in an eerie silence. It was almost, Joe thought, like the end of the world.

After checking to make sure Frank was all right, Joe led the way back into the control room. Every piece of equipment had been destroyed, either by exploding or being smashed by flying pieces of metal and glass. Small fires burned in several spots along the consoles. Joe eyed them nervously. With all this electronic equipment, who knew what might spark into a serious blaze?

"Kareem," Frank said, "are you guys all right?"

Slowly Kareem and his three fellow workers crawled out from beneath the consoles. "Wow,"

Kareem said, surveying the damage. "I never saw one in action before. It really makes you think."

"Where's Paulette?" one of the other technicians asked. "Did she manage to get away before her screamers went off?"

"Paulette's gone," Frank said. "There's no time to look for her now. We need to secure this place against a major fire. Come on, Joe. We'll call the police and fire department from downstairs."

"I'm sure they're on their way now," Kareem said. "Believe me, nobody watches over its property with more enthusiasm than Evanco—especially since the kidnapping. Security must have seen the explosion on the monitors downstairs."

Just then the sound of running feet reached the group from the stairs. "See?" said Kareem.

Joe turned to his brother and said in a low voice, "After we talk to the police, we need to find Dad and let him know what happened. Then, let's go talk to Laird."

"Whatever you say," Frank agreed. "But I doubt even this disaster will change Laird's mind."

Half an hour later, Frank left the police, the fire department, and the four quickly recovering technicians to find their father in the employees' dining room. But this time, he was nowhere to be found.

"Maybe he heard about the explosion and is

on his way to the top floor to see if we're there," Joe suggested.

"You're probably right," said Frank. "If so, Kareem will tell him we're okay. Why don't we go straight to Laird's office now? Lieutenant Babain will probably show up after the control center fiasco, and once she gets here she'll take up all of Laird's time."

"Aye, aye, Captain," Joe said cheerfully, grabbing a breakfast roll from a nearby basket on their way out of the room. They took the elevator down, then went to the other elevator bank, where they rode up to the executive office floor.

"May I help you boys?" The receptionist asked when she saw the Hardys get off the elevator.

"Mr. Laird, please," Frank said.

"Excuse me—is he expecting you?" the woman asked.

"Yes," Joe said, chewing on his roll as he walked past her.

"Just a minute!" The receptionist got up and hurried to place herself between Joe and the hallway that led to Laird's office. "Have a seat over there," she commanded both the boys. "I'll buzz Mr. Laird and see if he's free."

With a sigh, both the Hardys sat down to wait. "I hate this," Joe said, tearing off a piece of his roll and handing it to Frank. "Wherever you go, people in offices always make you wait."

"I know what you mean," Frank said. He lowered his voice so that the receptionist couldn't hear him. "But I'll tell you something. This time I don't feel like waiting."

Joe popped the last of the roll into his mouth and nodded. "Neither do I," he said quietly. "At the count of three?"

"One," Frank murmured, his eyes on the hallway. "Two. Three!"

In a single movement, both Hardys stood and raced down the hallway. The receptionist jumped to her feet again, shouting as the boys reached the door to Bruno Laird's office and opened it.

"Hello, boys."

"The man with the eyepatch," Joe said to Frank.

"The one and only." The man in the rubber mask grinned evilly at the Hardys. In his hand was the same gun he had used when kidnapping Sarah. But Joe saw with a quick glance around the room that Sarah wasn't there this time. No one was in the office but the man with the eyepatch and the tall, burly man who'd helped him before.

"Hi there, Seethus," Joe said.

The tall man stared at Joe, then at his accomplice.

"Ignore them," the man with the eyepatch snapped. He aimed his gun first at Joe, then at Frank. "All right, you two," he growled, his voice sinister. "You've played around enough at Evanco's expense. It's time to go for a little ride."

As the man with the eyepatch ushered the

boys back into the reception area, he kept his gun hidden in Joe's side. Exchanging a friendly nod with the receptionist, the man and his accomplice waited for the elevator. When it arrived, the foursome stepped in.

On the way down, Joe watched the man with the eyepatch tug at the lobe of his ear. "I thought it was you," Joe said calmly. "First Bruno Laird, then J. P. Evans, then the scientist in the technology museum, and now this. That mask-making software you guys have been using is amazing stuff. But which character is the real you?"

"Shut up and maybe you'll live longer," the kidnapper growled.

The elevator reached the lobby, and the doors slid open. "Now march," said the man with the eyepatch. "Remember—my gun's right here in my pocket. And don't think I won't use it if I have to."

The gunmen escorted Frank and Joe out of the building and down the street to where a small, nondescript gray truck with the Evanco logo stood parked on the curb. After pushing the boys into the back of the truck, the men locked the door. Frank and Joe sat facing each other as the kidnappers climbed into the cab of the truck and drove away.

"That was a good question," Frank remarked. He could just make out Joe's outline in the darkness of the truck. "Which character *is* the real one? Evans? Laird? Ludwig? Eyepatch, even?"

"I've been thinking about it," Joe said. "I

figure the easiest way to answer that is to start by asking which one would benefit the others most if he happened to disappear?''

"Hmm." Frank frowned, trying to concentrate. "J. P. Evans, maybe," Frank said at last. "He controls everything at Evanco, after all. Imagine if one of his employees woke up one day and decided he could run the company a lot more easily without J.P. He could kidnap the boss, then use those miracle masks to impersonate him the few times he really had to."

"Of course, he couldn't fool everyone with a mask," Joe said slowly. "But with a guy as eccentric and isolated as J.P. is, it would be easier than with most. Really, the only people who might know for sure that J.P. had been replaced by an impostor would be J.P.'s bodyguard—and it looks like Seethus is in on this scam—and his daughter, Sarah."

"So what's the solution?" Frank said excitedly. "Kidnap Sarah, of course. Now you have no one who can control what you do. And who would be in a position to want that kind of power?"

The brothers said at the same time, "Bruno Laird."

It wasn't long before the van ride ended. Frank and Joe were escorted out at gunpoint to find themselves at the Museum of Technology and Science's loading dock. Joe saw that a truck had just unloaded, and the door to the museum stood half-open. There was no one in sight, however.

"This way," the man with the eyepatch ordered, nudging Joe toward the door with the muzzle of his gun. The foursome entered the museum, then immediately descended a flight of stairs to the maintenance area below. Joe eyed his kidnapper, trying to see the face of J. P. Evans as it had looked in the back of the limousine. But the man in the costume shop had been right—if the builds of Evans, Laird, Ludwig, and the eyepatch man hadn't been the same, he never would have believed they were all the same man.

The screamers had started everything, Joe realized as he and Frank were escorted down a corridor. Laird had probably gone crazy when Evans decided to give up the program in favor of reuniting with his daughter. Perhaps he had ordered Kareem to set off a few screamers himself to throw the detectives off his trail. And perhaps Paulette had programmed more than she had admitted—and had no intention of stopping until Laird did.

"In here," the eyepatch man said brusquely, knocking Joe to the left with the gun. "Sorry to have to leave you here," he taunted them as Frank and Joe entered a small, dimly lit room. "You'll miss the first full-scale screamer demonstration. We've had our trial runs in the past few weeks, but now it's time to really let loose."

As he spoke, the other man pulled impatiently at his mask. Joe watched, fascinated, as the realistic-looking false skin was torn away to reveal the face of Conrad Seethus.

"Yeah," Seethus added with a sneer. "Sayonara, little boys. We have to get ready for the last day of Evanco's little security seminar. Someone we all know is going to demonstrate a computerized suspect background search for police use. It's going to blow sky-high."

Joe turned to look at his brother. By Frank's sudden pallor, Joe knew his brother and he were thinking the same thought. Their father would be at the seminar today. In fact, he was scheduled to give the demonstration!

Joe glared at their kidnappers. "You won't get away with this," he said.

Seethus laughed, as he wiped the last bits of rubber from his face. "That's what they all say. But then we do," he assured Joe.

"Goodbye, boys," said his partner as the pair backed out of the room. "Say hello to your friends. You won't be together long."

"What friends?" Frank asked as the brothers listened to the click of the lock in the door. "We don't have any friends here."

"You do now—at least I hope you do."

Joe spun around to see who was speaking. He stared in the dim light at two forms huddled beneath blankets in the darkest corner of the room.

"Sarah?" Joe said, moving closer to get a better look at the girl.

"Right," Sarah said tersely. "Believe me, I'm as surprised to see you here as you are to see me."

Joe's gaze moved from Sarah's pretty, defiant face to that of the older man beside her.

"Don't tell me," Joe said, staring at the man. "Mr. J. P. Evans himself."

The man nodded modestly. "In person. We were brought here during the night, after being held captive in a house somewhere outside Chicago. Now—how are you boys going to get us out of this awful place?"

"We just got here," Joe protested, scrutinizing the computer billionaire. He looked far saner in person than his reputation would lead anyone to believe.

"You hear that sound?" Frank asked.

Joe listened for a moment, until he caught a high, faint hum drifting into the room from the other side of the wall.

"What's over there?" Joe asked Sarah and her father. "Do you know?"

"Computers," Sarah said. "It's not just computers, though. It's screamers."

Joe looked at his brother. The sound seemed to be rising gradually in pitch, and growing louder. "Screamers?" he repeated.

"Big enough to punch through this wall," Sarah told him flatly. "An explosion like that would easily kill us all."

Chapter

14

SO THAT'S WHAT Seethus meant by "Sayonara," Frank thought as he frantically scanned the room for something with which to break down the door. They were in a storage room, surrounded by cans of paint thinner and piles of dirty rags. *Flammable* rags, Frank realized.

"The only way out is through the ventilator shaft," he said at last, walking over and inspecting the opening in the ceiling. "One of us could crawl through it to the next room and stop the screamers."

"Or we could try to escape the building that way," suggested Joe.

Evans nodded. "The program would be easy enough to stop if I could get to the keyboard next door."

Frank looked from Evans to the vent. "Could you get through there, do you think?"

Evans blanched. "I don't see how. Of course, our lives are at stake. . . ."

"I was afraid of that." Frank moved beneath the vent. "Joe, lift me up."

Joe joined his brother and locked his hands together as a step up. He boosted Frank high enough for the older Hardy to pry open the grating with his hotel room key. The grating tumbled to the floor.

"This is going to be tight," Frank said. He tried to ignore the increasing volume of the hum next door as he pulled himself into the shaft.

Frank could see that the distance to the next vent was only a few feet. He squirmed forward and peered down at the room next door. It was a small business office, with ledgers open on several tables and a computer system on the desk.

Frank slapped out the grating from the vent with his hand, then squirmed backward and reached through the storage-room vent to help his brother up. "Hurry," he said. "That hum isn't getting any softer."

"We're going to try the door first," Frank called back to the others. Then he squirmed forward again, knocked out the grille of the computer room vent, and dropped to the floor. By the time Joe landed, Frank had discovered that this room, too, was locked.

"We'll just have to disarm the computer, then," Frank said as he stared at the machine.

"Let's pull the plug," Joe suggested.

Frank checked the plug and shook his head. "We can't do it without a blowtorch," he pointed out. "The connections run directly into the wall, without a socket, and the cords are shielded in metal casing."

"Okay," Joe said, his eyes darting nervously around the room. "What next?"

"Mr. Evans!" Frank moved toward the ventilation shaft and called into the next room. "To disarm the computer, what do we do first?"

Frank motioned for Joe to stand near the vent and listen for instructions while he himself returned to the computer to carry them out.

"Get to the menu," Joe translated to his brother. "Once you're there, look for something that cuts off a local loop or blocks intersystem communications."

"What?" Frank's fingers flew on the keyboard.

Joe asked Evans for an explanation. Then he said to Frank, "We're going to try to interrupt the program as it runs."

Joe continued relaying Evans's instructions while Frank executed them. Meanwhile, the ringing grew louder in Frank's ears. He tried to ignore the fact that he was right in front of the computer, typing away on a time bomb. But it was the only way any of them would get out of there alive, he reasoned—and the only way to save their father from the screamer attack scheduled for the demonstration.

"Just hit it," Frank heard Joe say through the static of his own thoughts.

"What?" Frank looked at his brother, blinking.

"Four! Hit option four!" Joe yelled.

Frank first pressed the number four, then the Enter key, and then Field Exit, causing the computer to skip a screen. A mass of numbers appeared at the top of the screen, glowing green against the black background.

Suddenly the pitch of the computer's scream shifted. Frank tried to remember Evans's last instruction, but the computer was screaming so loud that he knew there was no more time. He had to type something, *anything*, or the room would explode. "Get down!" he yelled at Joe. Then, closing his eyes, he jammed his finger onto a key.

Silence followed. Frank stood with his eyes closed, waiting for the explosion. But nothing happened. Finally Frank opened his eyes and read from the computer screen, " 'Screamer temporarily aborted. Press any key to continue overload/explosion sequence.' "

They were still alive.

"That was too close." Frank backed away from the computer. Joe moved closer to take a peek, but Frank barred the way. "Let's figure out how to get that door open," Frank said, wiping the sweat from his forehead.

"Won't Seethus and the other guys be expecting an explosion?" Joe asked.

"If they do, they sure wouldn't wait around for it," Frank pointed out. "They're long gone by now."

Using the tip of a metal bookend wedged between the door and the frame, Frank and Joe forced the office door's lock. The door sprang open, and the Hardys next forced open the storage closet down the hallway.

"We need to hurry," Evans said. "After five minutes the program may recycle and explode anyway."

"Follow me. I got out of here once before," Joe said, leading the way.

Frank brought up the rear as the group hurried down the deserted tunnel. When they reached an intersection, Joe motioned to the others to continue straight ahead. Just when Frank thought the corridor would stretch on forever, the group reached a door that led to a staircase, which appeared to lead up to the main floor.

Joe had just put a foot down on the first step, however, when the lower level was rocked by an explosion.

"Hit the ground!" Frank yelled, pulling Sarah down ahead of him. He looked up just in time to see a flash of fire stretch the length of the corridor. A series of fire alarms went off as several smaller explosions followed. Frank thought of the paint thinner in the storage room and shuddered. Then the basement sprinkler system sprang to life, instantly drenching all four escapees with water.

"Get moving," Joe cried.

Joe, Frank, and the Evanses pushed through gathering smoke from the basement up to the gallery level. Operating hours were in effect, and museum guests milled about in confusion. "Attention, patrons," said a voice over a loud-speaker. "Please walk to the nearest exit. Do not run."

"Come on," Frank said to Joe. "We have to find a phone and call Dad. Or if we can't reach him, we need to talk to Lieutenant Babain. She's the only one with enough authority to stop the seminar!"

But Frank discovered that all the phones were out at the museum, due to the underground fire. "Let's go there ourselves," Joe said to him. "We have J. P. Evans himself with us. He can stop the seminar, disarm the screamers, and tell everyone assembled what's been going on."

Frank agreed, and the brothers quickly rounded up Sarah and her father. After running outside, they searched frantically for a cab. Frank stood on the curbside, clenching and unclenching his fists.

"Hey," Sarah said, looking up at the sky. "What's going on?"

Frank followed her gaze. A helicopter was approaching the museum parking lot. As a pair of fire trucks and several police cars arrived, the helicopter settled down a short distance from the Hardys. Frank peered through the window to see Paulette in the passenger's seat.

Frank's spirits lifted instantly as he ran to the chopper, followed by Joe, Sarah, and her father.

"How'd you know where we were?" he asked Paulette as he climbed into the back of the helicopter.

"I followed you," Paulette confessed, shouting over the noise of the rotors and the fire engines. A crowd of people had gathered around the museum and were creating their own noise as well. "I wanted to know what you were up to. I thought you were after me. I saw you leave the lobby with Sarah's kidnappers, and I followed you here. You disappeared into the museum, and I couldn't find you, so I called the airport and hired this chopper. I figured if I was going to help out with the great escape, I might as well make it dramatic."

"Sarah!" the girl exclaimed when she saw her roommate running toward her. "You're okay!"

"You've saved us, Paulette," Sarah said. "We have to get back to the Evanco Building right away. The kidnappers planted a screamer at the seminar. If we don't stop the virus immediately, it will blow up the whole second floor."

Paulette hesitated.

"No, Paulette, we don't want Daddy's building to blow up," Sarah admonished her. "He and I had plenty of long talks while we were locked up together. We both had a lot of explaining to do. But I'm sure you'll understand a lot of what he did in the past—especially considering what you've been up to lately."

Paulette ducked her head in embarrassment. Then she motioned to everyone to crowd into the chopper. "Sorry, Mr. Evans," she said grimly as the older man was forced to share the passenger seat in the front. "I know how much you hate being in close contact with other people, with their germs and all. But I could only afford one chopper.''

"It's all right, I suppose,'' Evans said. "To tell you the truth, I've had about enough of all that myself. Sarah has shown me how ridiculous my life has become lately.'' He leaned past Paulette to take a better look at the pilot. "Aren't you the man who was tied up by the kidnappers and tossed in the back of your helicopter?'' he asked.

"Sangmin Lee, at your service, sir,'' the pilot said with a salute. "And here we go . . .''

The chopper lifted effortlessly into the cold winter air. As it moved over the city toward the Evanco Building, Joe leaned forward toward Mr. Evans. "Shouldn't we radio your building and tell them what's happening?'' he asked. "Maybe they can stop the screamers before we get there.''

"Not a chance,'' Paulette protested. "Radioing in would only alert Laird and the others to the fact that you've gotten free. I say it's better to take them by surprise. The last thing we want is for Laird to think his plans are unraveling,'' Paulette pointed out. "He might decide to roll his Doomsday Tapes.''

"What are those?'' Frank frowned. He didn't like the sound of them at all.

"They're a mass broadcast of a delayed screamer program to every computer on the EXacT network, with each computer passing the virus along to every other network it's tied into. Fully activated, the Doomsday Tapes might even start a war—or, at the very least, kick off a major stock market crash.''

Frank stared at J. P. Evans. "How could you hire someone to write a program like that?"

A silence followed. Then Paulette said sheepishly, "He didn't. I wrote it at school, for extra credit."

Shaking his head in dismay, Frank looked down and saw that the helicopter was circling the Evanco Building's rooftop landing pad but was unable to land. An Evanco security guard stood in the center of the pad, shooting up at them.

The pilot ducked instinctively with every shot, but the shots missed the helicopter entirely. "What's going on?" J.P. demanded, trying to see below.

"Apparently Seethus and Laird have your security people well under control," Frank answered, pointing at the man.

"I'm not surprised," J.P. said dryly. "Try to land anyway," he told the pilot. "When they see it's me, they'll back off in a hurry."

Frank wasn't so sure, but he kept quiet as the pilot banked the helicopter so that the force of the rotors began to blow a huge wind down at the gunman. Frank watched the wind throw the man off balance. Then he saw another guard pick up a firehose and start spraying water at the chopper.

"What's he doing?" Frank demanded, peering down at the man. Then he realized that in the freezing weather the water would quickly turn to ice.

Suddenly the helicopter started to shake as ice formed on the spinning rotors. As the helicopter fell away from the building, Sarah screamed, "We're going to crash!"

Chapter

15

"I'VE GOT TO get away from the water!" Joe heard Lee shout. The pilot had moved the chopper back away from the building to avoid a collision, but now they were beside the great glass tower, going down. Clutching his seat belt, Joe felt his stomach rise. A hundred and twenty floors, he reminded himself. Straight down! He sat back, trying not to watch. Sarah, who sat next to him, was staring determinedly at her feet. Frank gazed nervously down at the street, far below.

Suddenly Joe felt a new sensation. "We're not going down any more," he said. "We're hovering again."

The pilot tossed a grin at them over his shoulder. "Nice view, eh?" he said.

Joe looked out to see people gathered at their

office windows, staring at the helicopter. "Will we be able to land?" Joe heard J. P. Evans ask.

"We'll get there," Lee replied. "That was a close call, though. Not enough water hit the rotors to make us go down. I'll come in with the wind to keep them from soaking my rotors."

Lee turned back to his controls and flew the helicopter around the Evanco Building. As the chopper turned the corner of the building, the pilot pulled its nose up. The helicopter climbed, swinging around the building's northwest corner.

"Don't hit the building!" J. P. Evans yelled. "It's not paid for yet."

"Don't worry," the pilot answered. The chopper broke over the top of the skyscraper, clearing the roof. Joe looked down to see the two gunmen still there.

"It's showtime," Lee whooped, angling the helicopter forward. The blast from the rotors knocked both gunmen back against the skyscraper's roof. "How about a haircut, guys?" he yelled. Joe stared out the window as Lee nudged the chopper lower, then settled it onto the landing pad.

"Wow." Joe let out his breath for the first time in several minutes. "That was some touchdown." He saw the two gunmen bolt toward the control center's door.

"Lee, get this chopper back to the airport safe and sound," Paulette said, reaching past J. P. Evans to swing open the door. "Thanks a lot for your help—you've been great today." She turned toward the backseat and commanded, "The rest of you guys, come on!"

Paulette led the way into the control center. As he entered, Joe saw that the room had been abandoned and that the guards were nowhere in sight. The debris had been swept up, but no technicians remained with the damaged, dented equipment.

"Not a good sign," Frank said to his brother.

Joe agreed. He watched J. P. Evans stride directly to the telephone, dial a number, and begin barking orders into the receiver. Joe overheard him say, "No one can be trusted inside the company from now on, and I mean nobody, Lindquist! Get all our security people out of the building. And I want the police here, on the double. And call the FBI. I'm upstairs in EXacT's control center. I'll wait for you to report back here."

Evans hung up. "What I need is Taylor Hayes," he said half to himself. "*There* was a man I could depend on to put things back together."

He was interrupted by a cry of frustration from Paulette. Joe turned to see that Paulette and Frank had commandeered one of the less-battered computer consoles and were working madly to shut down the EXacT system relays before they went through to the connected computers. "Too late!" Paulette cried, leaning her head against the console in frustration. She turned to Evans. "The first download already went through!"

Evans nodded, his face grim. "I suppose that means the second-floor conference rooms are set to blow."

"But you said you could stop it!" Joe said to Paulette.

"We tried," Frank told his brother, "but they ran the program before we got here."

"Then maybe we should knock out the satellite dishes," Sarah suggested.

"It's too late for that," Paulette said impatiently. "The screamer is already buried in the memory of the crime control network that Mr. Hardy is supposed to demonstrate. It has to be stopped downstairs, in the computer itself. And even then I'm not sure there's time."

"There are dozens of people down there about to be killed," Joe reminded them. "Let's go."

"You're right." Frank headed for the stairs.

"Wait for me," Paulette cried. "I know how to stop the stupid thing."

As she left the room, Joe saw Paulette glance over her shoulder at J. P. Evans. Joe remembered that J.P. had learned how to stop the screamer, too. But at the moment, Joe realized, the executive was too weighed down with trying to save his company to help Paulette unless it was absolutely necessary.

It doesn't matter, Joe told himself. Paulette invented the screamers. She can certainly stop them. He hurried to catch up with Frank and the girl.

"Wait for me!" Sarah cried, running after them. At the stairs, she turned for a last look at her father. "Are you sure you'll be okay up here, Daddy?" she asked.

"Of course," Evans growled. "I'm always okay when I'm in this building. It's out in the real world that I run into trouble."

Sarah smiled fondly at him. Then she raced downstairs with Joe to where the rest of the group waited impatiently for the elevator.

It was easy for Frank to find the conference room where Fenton Hardy was scheduled to demonstrate the new police records system: All the sessions in the seminar had been held on the second floor, and Frank was able to follow the sound of his father's voice to the proper room.

"Excuse me," Frank said loudly, interrupting Fenton Hardy in midsentence as he and the others barged into the conference room. Frank saw that nearly fifty people were crowded into the room, taking notes as Mr. Hardy spoke.

Mr. Hardy frowned as his son strode to the front of the room. After Frank had explained in a low voice what was going on, his father looked even grimmer. "Jim, Trisha, Bill," he said, turning to members of the audience seated in the front row, "we're going to need your help. It's very important."

The rest of the audience murmured restlessly as the three people Fenton had called stepped to the front of the room.

"What's going on?" the woman named Trisha asked.

"Maybe nothing," Mr. Hardy said quietly.

"On the other hand, there's a possibility we may have to evacuate the floor, as a precaution."

Paulette ran over to the terminal Mr. Hardy was using to demonstrate the police records network.

"Where's the keyboard?" Paulette demanded. "The input?"

"Right here," Fenton told her, stepping back to reveal the computer terminal.

She sat down at the computer and started typing. Meanwhile, Fenton and the three adults he'd picked began to quietly evacuate the room.

After the rest of the seminar participants had left, whispering among themselves and darting curious glances at the young people surrounding Paulette, Mr. Hardy returned to the front of the room and asked Frank in a low voice, "Are you sure this one's on our side?"

Frank glanced at Paulette, who scowled darkly at the computer screen while her hands flew across the keyboard. "Sure I'm sure," Frank said. "If our lives are saved today, it will be mostly due to her."

"Maybe we should back up a little, just in case," Mr. Hardy said. They all moved back until they were well out of the way of the computer. Paulette continued typing, unaware of the goings-on around her. Frank watched, impressed. He could now see the side of Paulette her fellow programmers were awed by. It wasn't every day he had the chance to watch a programming whiz in action.

"Will it make that humming sound if it's about to blow?" Sarah asked uncertainly.

"I guess so," Frank answered. "None of the other computers exploded without that sound."

To Frank's horror, his last few words were buried under a soft but persistent hum emanating from the computer at the front of the room. The entire group turned in one movement to stare at the machine. Paulette, Frank noticed, seemed oblivious to the danger as she continued typing commands into the keyboard.

"We're out of here!" Joe cried as the hum grew louder and higher. "Run for it!"

"Wait!" Paulette yelled, still typing. Frank felt his body twitch, caught between the urge to run and the urge to stay and protect Paulette. Fenton Hardy was already pulling Sarah toward the door. Joe was hanging back a little, waiting for Frank to join them.

"Paulette!" Frank shouted, not wanting to leave the girl there. "Come on! It's too late!"

"Just thirty seconds," she replied. Frank watched her wrestle with the computer virus, beads of perspiration appearing on her brow as the hum switched into a high-pitched whistle, as loud as a teakettle on full boil.

"Fifteen more seconds!" Paulette promised, typing even faster. Suddenly, to Frank's great relief, the whistle stopped abruptly. The conference room was filled with nothing but silence.

"I did it!" Paulette looked up at Frank and smiled. The others, weak with amazement and relief, moved toward her to offer their congratulations.

But before they could reach Paulette, Frank's ears were bombarded with a sickeningly familiar sound.

The computer had exploded, right in Paulette's face!

Chapter

16

"PAULETTE!" Joe heard Sarah scream as the glass spattered the area around Paulette. The dark-haired girl was bent over in her chair, clutching her face and moaning.

"Call an ambulance!" Joe ordered as he and the others rushed toward Paulette. Gently he lifted Paulette's head to see tiny rivers of blood running down her face.

"It doesn't look too bad," Mr. Hardy comforted the girl as Frank called for emergency medical help. "You have a few superficial cuts, but the paramedics should be able to deal with them."

"I was lucky," Paulette said. She accepted a handkerchief from Mr. Hardy and dabbed at her cuts, then gingerly pulled a sliver of glass from above her eye. "I should have realized that such an enormous power buildup would have to exit somewhere, even if I did stop the program in time."

"You were great, Paulette," Sarah said loyally. "If not for you, every terminal on this floor would have blasted to pieces—to say nothing of the people sitting in front of them."

"Think about it," Frank remarked. "All those people working away, unaware that their lives may have just been saved."

The door flew open, and Kareem Addar appeared on the threshold. "Hi, everyone!" he said excitedly. "Didn't you hear, the building's being evacuated!"

"Too late for that," Paulette said. "By the way, Kareem, someone needs to correct a design flaw in the virus program—namely, that even after you stop it, sometimes the computer explodes, anyway."

Kareem blanched when he saw that Paulette had been hurt. "Wow," he said, coming closer. "Is that the reason for the evacuation? I swear, I had nothing to do with this, Paulette. Nothing!"

"Nobody's going to have anything to do with the screamer virus from now on," Mr. Hardy stated. "Fortunately for everyone, transmitting computer viruses is illegal in this country. You can bet the first thing I'll do after we get Paulette bandaged up is see to it that screamers are never heard from again."

"You're right, Mr. Hardy," Paulette said slowly. "I thought screamers were my chance at the big time. I really blew it."

"Hey, Paulette, who says chances come only once in a lifetime?" Kareem chided her. "Besides, I bet designing video games is more fun than trying to destroy as many computers as possible in the shortest conceivable time."

"Speak for yourself, Kareem," Joe remarked stiffly.

"I *am* speaking for myself!" the programmer replied. "That explosion in the control center really got me thinking. Do I want to spend my life writing programs like that? Since the answer is no, I've decided to quit my job, look for financing, and start my own video game company. How about it, Paulette? Want to work with me?"

"Well, that depends," Paulette said shyly. "Can Sarah sign up, too?"

"I may not be a computer genius like you two," Sarah pointed out quickly. "But I have the bucks to finance a couple of geniuses like you. My only requirements are that educational games be donated to any school that asks for them. You guys are free to make a profit on the junkier ones, though."

The group of young people stood around, grinning at one another, as J. P. Evans strode into the room. "What's this?" he asked, holding his arms out to the huddled group. "The evacuation's over, the virus is destroyed. I come downstairs to thank you all, and I find you plotting something!"

"Nothing you wouldn't be proud of, Dad,"

Sarah said with a smile. "We're just founding a second-generation communications industry."

J.P. looked mystified. With a shrug, he turned to the Hardys, and his expression turned hard again. "I thought you'd like to know that Laird and Seethus were arrested running out into the street half an hour ago. Their arrest will no doubt make a major difference in my life, and in the condition of this company. I decided I owe you boys an explanation."

"Great," Joe said, pulling up a chair. "To start with, who *is* Bruno Laird, really? And what is his connection to Dr. Ludwig?"

"That's a good question," Evans replied with a sigh. "The answer makes for a long story. I should start by saying that back in the forties, Dr. Ludwig was *the* leader in computer research in the country, if not the world. He was still very young then—barely out of his teens—and extremely reclusive. Though all of us in the newborn computer industry had read his papers, almost none of us had ever seen his face."

"Yes?" Frank said, taking a chair next to Joe as all the others in J.P.'s audience followed suit. "So then what?"

"So then came the fifties," J.P. said gravely, sitting down himself, "and he lost all his money. Ludwig was being blackmailed by someone. I never found out by whom, or why. But in any case, he got so desperate for work that I finally offered him a job—if he agreed to work under a false name."

"A name like Bruno Laird?" Joe said.

"Exactly." Evans crossed his legs. "Ludwig—or Laird—worked with me for nearly forty years. He led a kind of double life, and he managed to win a great reputation for Ludwig while at the same time helping to make Evanco a multimillion-dollar corporation. And no one ever recognized Laird for who he really was."

"Wow," Paulette said with a glance at Kareem. "Then why did he turn against you?"

"He wanted power," Evans said simply. "More power, that is. I knew that as Dr. Ludwig, Laird had invented a fantastic program for designing facial masks. What I didn't know was that he was using the program to devise more identities for himself.

"When screamers came along, Laird found the virus irresistible," Evans continued. "When I demanded that he get rid of the program, he found it easier to dispose of me—and my daughter—than to let go of it. After all," Evans said with a wistful expression, "he'd known me for so many years. He probably looked forward to impersonating me whenever he had the chance."

In the stunned silence that followed, Kareem asked, "What are you going to do now, Mr. E?"

"Develop an antivirus for the screamers as soon as possible," Evans announced. "In fact, an old friend of mine might be persuaded to help me with that, now that Mr. Laird is gone for good."

"Taylor Hayes?" Frank asked.

"That's the one," Evans answered. "I've

called the hospital, and apparently he's doing fine. I'll make him a job offer this afternoon.''

"What about Laird, Dad?" Sarah asked. "Will he be charged with fraud?"

"Kidnapping, to start with," Evans said. "And after that, attempted murder, I suppose. Mr. Laird can expect to be in prison for a long, long time."

"Hi, kids."

The group turned in their chairs to see Lieutenant Gabriella Babain and Officer Adler standing out in the hall.

The lieutenant said cheerfully, "Just thought I'd check in and let you know we have the two major culprits safely in jail, as well as two guards. The kidnapping's been solved, the bad guys have been caught, and Adler and I are both up for a raise. And I have to admit, Frank and Joe, we owe most of that to you."

"Great," Joe said with a grin. "Next time you interrogate us, Lieutenant, maybe you could give us a little more benefit of the doubt."

"You mean, loosen up on the job? Over my dead body." Babain made the rounds of the room, shaking hands warmly with each person there.

"I'll tell you what," Sarah said, jumping to her feet in her excitement. "Why don't we have a party before Frank and Joe have to go home? We have a lot to celebrate—my rescue, Laird's arrest, Paulette's and Kareem's and my new company."

"And last but not least," Evans said, standing

up and putting an arm around his daughter, "the long-awaited reunion of a young woman and her dad."

Joe cheered and clapped his hands above his head. "It had better be a costume party," he said. "If there's one thing I know about Chicago by now, it's where to find the greatest disguises in the world."

"I'm with you," Frank said, joining his brother. "And you know one thing we're not going to disguise ourselves as?"

Joe looked at his brother. The two of them grinned, and in one voice said, "Bruno Laird!"

Frank and Joe's next case:

Somebody's ripping off rap artist Randy Rand by counterfeiting copies of his hottest tunes and cutting in on his profits. For Frank and Joe, the case is a piece of cake. The trail leads right to a hustler named Jack Martinelli, and the Hardys catch the con man in the act. But the act turns downright dirty when Martinelli turns up dead!

Suddenly rapper Randy faces a murder rap—and the Hardy boys face deadly danger on the mean streets of New York. They're convinced the real killer is running free, and it's up to them to do their stuff—no matter how rough it gets. Because if they don't find the dude who did the deed, cool man Randy Rand will soon be cooling his heels in jail . . . in *Bad Rap,* Case #73 in The Hardy Boys Casefiles™.